Forever Bound

Books by Kallypso Masters

Rescue Me Saga (Erotic Military Romance)

Kally has no intention of ending the *Rescue Me Saga* ever, but will continue to introduce spinoff series in the years to come. The following *Rescue Me Saga* titles are available in e-book and print formats on my website and at major booksellers:

Masters at Arms & Nobody's Angel (Combined Volume)
Nobody's Hero
Nobody's Perfect
Somebody's Angel
Nobody's Lost
Nobody's Dream
Somebody's Perfect

Rescue Me Saga Box Set Books 1-3 (e-book only)
Rescue Me Saga Box Set Books 4-6 and Western Dreams (e-book only)

Rescue Me Saga Extras (Erotic Romance)

Novellas and Collections featuring couples from the *Rescue Me Saga*.
Western Dreams (Rescue Me Saga Extras #1)
(read chronologically between Nobody's Dream & Somebody's Perfect)
Wedding Dreams (Rescue Me Saga Extras #2)
(read chronologically after Somebody's Perfect)
Forever Bound (Rescue Me Saga Extras #3)
(read chronologically after Wedding Dreams, but best after Matteo: Wild Fire)

Raging Fire Series
(Steamy Firefighter Romance)

Angelina's firefighter brothers are getting their stories told!

TONY: Slow Burn

MATTEO: Wild Fire

FRANCO: Flashover (Raging Fire #3) is being serialized on Kally's Patreon fan page and will be released in novel form in 2022. RAFE, the fourth and final book in the series will be released in 2023.

Roar
(a *Rescue Me Saga* Erotic Romance Spin-off)

(Erotic Romance with secondary characters from the *Rescue Me Saga.) Roar* provides a lead-in to the upcoming trilogy with Patrick's, Grant's, and Gunnar's stories.)

Bluegrass Spirits

(Supernatural Contemporary Romance…with a Haunting Twist)

Jesse's Hideout

Kate's Secret

kallypsomasters.com/books

Forever Bound

(Rescue Me Saga Extras #3)

Scenes Beyond the HEAs of
Adam & Karla
Damián & Savannah
Ryder & Megan
Luke & Cassie

Kallypso Masters

Dedication

To my loyal fans who never tire of reading about these characters and allow me to come back to visit them too on occasions like this.

Acknowledgements

This **Forever Bound** collection of Rescue Me Saga extra scenes was made richer by my having met **Freya and Nevertheless** at a KallypsoCon 2021 tour of the Woodshed club in Orlando. My thanks also to **Master Cecil and Darcy** for opening the Woodshed doors to my attendees and featured authors for that special evening. Some parts of the suspension scenes in this book are directly from the videos I took of Freya and Never's demos. And Freya also was a big help in lots of e-mails back and forth making sure I described them in a safe and accurate way.

I want to thank my editor, **Meredith Bowery**, who always keeps an eye on my continuity issues with past books and lets me know what works and doesn't work as far as pacing, content, and emotional levels.

My thanks to my awesome alpha and beta readers—**Cassie Colton, TeraLe Durant, Annette Elens, Barb Jack, Gina Marcantonio, Carmen Messing, Lisa Simo-Kinzer**, and **Elaine Swinney**—for saving me from embarrassing errors and for helping me give my readers the best possible experience. Lisa, thanks always for your help on the PTSD issues and to you and Carmen, on the child development ones!

Thank you to my **Facebook The Rescue Me Saga Discussion Group**, for your advice and feedback on content questions, and for your enthusiasm for this latest installment.

Thanks also to my last-minute proofreading angel **Rebecca J. Cartee** of **Editing by Rebecca**. It was great working with you again! Glad you enjoyed your time with Master Adam too!

Author's Note

It's been a while since we've gotten to see how Adam and Karla and the other original couples in the Rescue Me Saga have been doing. While Damian & Savannah and Marc & Angelina have had their stories updated within the last few years, and we've captured glimpses of the early couples in the Raging Fire series, I wanted to get back inside their heads for an intimate look at their continuing stories. And so **Forever Bound** was born!

If you're new to my books or haven't caught up with book seven in the Rescue Me Saga and the two earlier Rescue Me Saga Extras, please note that this collection is not a standalone and is filled with spoilers from earlier books as well as teasers from related series.

This collection is filled with entertaining, sexy glimpses into the lives of these couples. So sit back, pour yourself a glass of wine or a cuppa, and enjoy your visit with old friends.

For timely updates, sneak peeks at unedited excerpts, and much more, sign up for my e-mails!

Known trigger warnings: One character will be dealing with the aftermath of PTSD and others will be coping with infertility issues and whether they want to start a family by other means. I am working on making a trigger warning list for all my books to put on my website, but always check the author's notes for the main ones I'm aware of.

Enjoy!

Kally

Section One

Adam

"**A**dam! Grab Rori before she gets out the door and streaks the neighbors!"

Karla's frantic plea drifted down the stairs as Adam tore himself away from his surveillance screens of a downtown nightclub. Adam's VIP security agency had been hired to monitor the place in light of a string of arsons that had been happening over the last six months. Things appeared to be quiet at the moment—downtown at least.

Adam glanced toward his open home office door in time to see his butt-naked toddler daughter dash past. Her giggles made him smile, as always, but he'd better go after her. She'd become quite the escape artist lately. Where was that meek Sleeping Beauty they had named Aurora?

Hero charged after her, barking with excitement, but Adam couldn't be sure if he was herding her back to safety or in on this escape attempt. The dog had also probably been responsible for removing Rori's training pants, a favorite trick of his lately. The rescue puppy they'd adopted from Chance's litter at Luke and Cassie's took his role as protector very seriously, which made it difficult for Adam to be upset with the overgrown pup.

The triplets would be turning three next week, and he and Karla had their hands full whenever they were awake and on the move, so Hero sometimes helped there too. It had been a lot easier to contain them when they weren't walking or running everywhere. They'd had two years of success at corralling them, but as the kids grew older, there'd been some slip-ups in their system.

Like today's.

Adam pushed his chair away from his desk and picked up his pace a little as he entered the hallway. He found the front door wide open and one of the toddler chairs next to it, which was apparently how Rori had unlocked the door. If only Adam and his team could move as fast as one of his kids.

Outside, Hero's barking alerted him as to which direction Rori had run. "Aurora Casandra Montague, get your aaa…behind back in here!"

"Catch me, Daddy!" He couldn't help but smile at her taunt. Maybe she'd take over his security agency someday, going after the bad guys with her abundance of sass and energy. It sure would be a lot safer than being in the military or law enforcement.

Their neighbors must think Karla and he were the most inept parents ever born, but let *them* try and keep up with three mobile toddlers. Seeing that Rori had doubled back and was now chasing after Hero, who was headed back toward the house, Adam decided to hide behind a bush. As Rori ran past him, he scooped her up.

"Gotcha!"

The little girl squealed, squirming to free herself as he carried her back toward the house. Before he could get to the door, Pax made his escape with Karla in pursuit. Hero tore across the lawn after him. Maybe the dog was actually trying to help, because his barking distracted Pax who came toward Hero rather than the street.

Keeping up with these kids was like herding cats. Just when he started to wonder where Kate was, she came running after Karla. At least those two still had their clothes on.

He couldn't help but laugh at the spectacle his family presented, hoping their neighbors enjoyed the show and weren't horrified by these more and more frequent escapades. Kate was an easy catch for him, so he scooped her up with an arm around her belly and gripped her in a football hold as he turned to check on Karla's progress.

She had Pax in her arms and shook her head at Adam. "You're going to have to put your security team on the mission of making an escape-proof kids' room. I'm too old for this!"

"You're too old?" He had twenty-five years on her, and she was complaining?

"You heard me." Her glare told him he'd have to let any further response go until later. She didn't seem amused at his question.

Karla held the door for him, because she still had a free hand. Inside the foyer, Adam set the two girls on the floor while keeping ahold of their hands as Hero darted down the hall. The girls struggled to be set free. Karla flipped the dead bolt on the front door, and he made a mental note to add a slide bar lock to the inside of the door this week. Surely, the kids wouldn't be able to figure out how to open that for a few years, although he'd thought the deadbolt would have been more than effective against a three-year-old too.

Right now, though, Karla seemed stressed, and that was job one.

"Why don't I get the kids their lunch while you take a break, Kitten?"

"Would you?" That brought a smile to her beautiful face. "I've had this song running through my head all morning, and I'm afraid if I don't write it down immediately, I'll lose it."

Letting go of the girls, he took Pax from her and set him down beside them before giving Karla a kiss on the cheek. "Go upstairs. I've got this under control."

The stress from earlier lifted from her face, and she beamed at him. "Thank you so much, sweetheart!" She gave him a quick peck on the cheek and, without a backward glance, she took the stairs two at a time. Soon, he heard the door to her studio close.

"Okay, kids, what do you want for lunch?"

"Peanut butter!"

"Gwilled cheese!"

"Fwoot Woops!"

Adam shook his head. He thought triplets were supposed to think alike. "PBJs it is. Come on. Let's rustle up some grub." When the two who'd asked for something else didn't complain, he considered it a victory.

*   *   *

Karla

Karla's new indie album released last month, and she'd been spending a lot of her spare time—such as it was—on social media promoting it. Today, though, a new song had been nagging at her. While the triplets were eating lunch with Adam, she decided to go to her studio to jot down the lyrics running through her brain while she had the opportunity. She'd learned the hard way that putting off that step meant risking losing the words altogether.

While she'd never make it big until she could do live performances on a regular basis, she tried to content herself with online sales. Megan shot her music videos for SoundCloud and Karla's two albums and many singles were up for purchase on BandCamp and were making decent sales. Her fan following continued to grow steadily.

However, keeping up with the triplets had become a full-time job. Adam wasn't able to help as much now that his private security agency had begun to take off in the Denver area. She loved that Adam had found something to occupy his time and bring in more money after selling the Masters at Arms Club to Mistress Grant, but she missed having her creative time.

Most nights, Karla found herself on the edge of exhaustion,

missing those earlier days when the triplets had gone to bed before dark. She and Adam hadn't been able to spend as much intimate time together, either. Baby monitors had been a godsend in the beginning. Back then, they'd even been able to sneak upstairs to their play area, although they hadn't been able to do rope suspensions or anything that would take too much time to get out of in an emergency.

But those days were gone. She could barely get them to take naps in the afternoons, and once one of them awoke in the morning, the entire household was up and off to the races. Karla loved taking care of her babies' needs, but they ran her ragged. While Adam worked from home most of the time and helped when business was slow for him, the primary responsibility fell upon her.

And she was too tired most nights to even engage in the most vanilla forms of sex. That only compounded her feelings of guilt when she did take time to work on her own career. Unlike her meager income, Adam's agency and his military pension brought in enough money to pay the bills and allowed them to save for their kids to go to college, if they wanted. Karla's royalties didn't pay enough to hire someone to help with the kids while she worked.

At least they didn't have a mortgage, thanks to Marc's generous offer on their house and the price Mistress Grant had paid the founders of the Masters at Arms. The deal had given Adam, who held a larger share than the others, enough money to start his security firm as well as put some money away for the kids' college fund.

But she missed playing at the club. Who had time these days, though? Not them or the Orlandos, and Marc and Angelina lived two hours away and rarely came to Denver. Angelina's restaurant kept her busy, and Marc had become a paramedic, working for both the Aspen Corners and Breckenridge fire departments.

She missed seeing her friends, but everyone's lives had changed in the past few years. Adam and Karla would continue to earn money where they could and on their quiet nights, be able to reconnect with each other on an intimate level. Things would get easier when the triplets went to kindergarten, Karla reminded herself at least once a day.

Still, Karla couldn't help but miss doing bondage scenes with her skilled rigger. Adam could send her into subspace almost the moment he touched her with the soft ropes he still kept ready to use at all times.

Unfortunately, she could count on one hand the number of times she'd been tied up in the past year.

We need to arrange for a babysitter sometime soon!

As she sat at her desk, the words spilled out onto the pages of her notebook. She no longer wrote songs of despair and heartache but instead, ones more focused on hope, love, and the triumph over evil. This one was inspired by Savannah's winning justice over her evil father more than two years ago.

A soft rapping on the door brought her back to the present. She glanced at the clock to see that it was almost three-thirty. Where had the hours gone?

Karla jumped up and went to the door to open it and find Adam leaning against the doorjamb, his broad shoulders filling out his black Marine Corps T-shirt. His suggestive smile said he'd like to do bad things to her.

Don't I wish!

"Sorry to interrupt, Kitten, but I have to run downtown for an hour or two."

"The kids are down for their afternoon nap, but I'm living on borrowed time." Karla sighed. "Hopefully, they'll sleep long enough to not be cranky tonight."

"What time are Damián and Savannah coming?"

"I told them six."

"I should be back before then." He leaned in to give her a kiss, and she tried not to get swept up in the thoughts she'd just been having about Adam tying her up. She really needed to plan a date night for them—and soon!

But tonight, the Orlandos were coming for their third wedding anniversary. They'd insisted they were fine celebrating with their kids, but it made Karla wonder if perhaps they might also need a date night. But tonight would be geared around the kids.

Karla made her way to the kitchen to gather up her ingredients for the Instant Pot. This pressure cooker had to be the best gift her parents had ever given her. Adam had been the one to read about it somewhere and suggested they give one to her parents. Oddly enough, she and Adam had given her parents one first, but they loved it so much, they reciprocated. With it, Karla had begun to enjoy cooking for the first time in her life. She might never be a gourmet like Angelina, but this appliance helped her put tasty meals on the table. Adam even liked using it from time to time.

Tonight's corned beef and cabbage meal should be amazing. It had been a staple for her growing up in Chicago. Best of all, she could set the timer and go about her busy day. Undoubtedly, the kids would need her attention when they woke from their naps.

Karla's hand went to her day collar, the Black Hills gold choker Adam had presented to her during her private collaring on their honeymoon at his family's cabin in South Dakota. The collar and their sweet—most of the time—children were the most special gifts he'd given her, but he also loved bringing her flowers and once upon a time, kinky toys.

Heading back upstairs to check on the kids, she found them sound asleep in their toddler beds. The thought of taking a nap herself crossed her mind, but she should have done that rather than writing down the song playing in her head. Instead, she decided to set the table, peel potatoes and carrots, and cut the cabbage. Then she could just add them to the pot later while the meat rested.

Before returning to the kitchen, she grabbed her pen and paper in case she'd be able to work on her song a little longer in the peace and quiet.

* * *

Adam

Adam sat back down at his desk and picked up his coffee. Lukewarm. He set the mug back down and cued up the latest surveillance footage his cameras had recorded.

Whatever was happening at the downtown bar had Adam stumped, but he had no more answers now than he had before going down to check it out. Surveillance footage had picked up a shady-looking character two nights in a row loitering behind the nightclub. The owner couldn't identify the man on Adam's videos, but a waitress said he was the one who'd asked her what she thought about all the fires that had been set in and around Denver this year.

Zooming in on the suspicious part of last night's video, Adam leaned closer to the monitor to see if he could pick out any clues he might have missed.

In recent months, a number of business owners had hired Adam's firm for added protection from arson and other crimes, but the cameras at the nightclub had resulted in the best activity. Whoever the firebug was knew how to inflict maximum damage to property, given the coverage he'd seen on the most recent incidents. Figuring Victor Holmes, a local fire investigator he knew from the Masters at Arms Club, would tell Adam what types of behaviors to watch for, he'd contacted him yesterday. Victor had shared some general tips, but suggested he talk to Franco Giardano, the lead investigator on these fires. While Adam had met him at Marc and Angelina's wedding, he didn't know him as well as he did Victor.

If the arsonist continued to escalate in the size and scope of the fires he set, someone was going to get injured—or worse. So far, none of the fires had been at any of the properties Adam and his team provided security for, thank goodness.

If that man showed up on surveillance again tonight, though, Adam would be sure to notify law enforcement to get someone down there immediately. In the meantime, he'd have his team take turns doing drive-bys of this bar and some of the nearby properties, whether they were under contract with Adam or not.

"Mommeee! Pax hurt!" The urgency in Rori's voice blasted down the stairway.

Adam jumped up from his desk and took off at a run. He bounded up the stairs to find the triplets together in the bathroom with a pair of scissors in Rori's hand. Blood poured from a gash near Pax's temple at the hairline.

Adam lurched at Rori and removed the weapon from her hand. Where had she gotten those shears, and what was she trying to do with them? He stared down at the bloody scissors and froze. Sweat broke out on his forehead as he forced air into his lungs. A child screamed in his ear in a language he didn't recognize.

A dirty-faced little boy pointed half of a pair of broken scissors at him, ready to stab him if he came any closer.

Who the fuck was this kid?

The boy shouted at him in a language Adam couldn't make out, but clearly a threat to Adam's Marines.

"What's wr—" Karla's question ended mid-word as she scanned the small, enclosed area.

Adam grabbed onto the edge of the vanity as he grounded himself in the present, pushing whatever had triggered him back to the recesses of his mind.

"Girls, go to your room," Karla demanded.

At her abrupt tone, both girls began crying but made a beeline to their room. She gave Adam the side-eye before she ordered, "Get me some towels." Without waiting for him to move, Karla turned her attention to Pax and rushed to him.

"Pax, sweetie, what happened?"

After a few slow, deep breaths, Adam forced himself to focus on the scene before him and disengaged from the past. Sweat dotted Adam's forehead, chilling him in the air-conditioned room.

He hadn't seen any blood on Rori or Kate, but judging by the amount gushing from Pax's head, his injury seemed massive.

What the hell had happened in here?

"Towels, Adam!"

In all the commotion, the boy finally decided this was serious and began to bawl in earnest. Adam made out the words *cut* and *hair.* The boy's blood dripped off his chin and onto his Mickey Mouse shirt. Adam's gut churned at the sight, flashing between Pax and that boy with the broken shears.

"Adam, get some towels." Karla's firm but authoritative voice finally broke through to him.

Do something to help, shithead!

Finally aware of what to do, he opened the linen closet and pulled out two bath towels and brought them over to her.

"The smaller ones, Adam. It's not bleeding *that* badly." *Was she serious? There was blood all over the place.* "I just need to put some pressure on the side of his head to stem the blood flow."

Adam dropped those towels onto the floor and returned seconds later with two smaller ones.

"Get this one wet," she said as she took the other one from him. When he returned with one dripping wet, the other had already become half soaked with blood. Adam couldn't stomach the sight of his kid bleeding to death right before his eyes. And yet he hadn't been able to do a damned thing.

Thank God Karla had this under control.

"Want me to call 911?" Adam asked.

She gave him a look that told him that wasn't necessary. "He might need stitches, but first I want to control the bleeding. Let's just pack up the kids and head to the pediatric emergency department. Unless you want to stay here with the girls while I run Pax over there." How could she stay so calm?

Clearly, Karla didn't think he was in any shape to take charge of the situation—and she'd be right. But he couldn't let her drive. She needed to take care of Pax. "I'll get Kate and Rori downstairs and into the SUV. Will you be okay here?"

She pulled the towel back to show that blood still streamed down the wailing boy's face, then quickly put pressure on it again. "Go! We'll meet you at the car."

Adam's hands shook as he went to the bedroom where the girls were bawling their eyes out, as well.

Rori hiccupped as he hugged her and tried to stop her tears. "I hurted Pax."

"It was an accident." Clearly, the kids had gotten into something they shouldn't have. "He'll be fine. But we're going to take him to the hospital. He might need to get stitched up."

I hope that's the worst-case scenario, anyway.

Surely the cut was superficial, but his heart pounded as he took each girl by the hand and led them toward the stairs. He glanced inside the bathroom as they passed, but Karla had already packed up Pax and gone downstairs, apparently.

"Come on, girls. Double time."

Adam rushed toward the open front door, holding onto both of the girls. He might have lifted them into the air but hardly remembered his own feet touching the stairs.

Karla was already in the driver's seat. His wife had everything under control. She even had Pax holding a towel against the side of his own head, although the kid removed it for a moment to show the girls, which made them both scream and start to cry louder.

"Pax, keep that towel where Mommy told you to," he admonished.

Fighting the urge to pull Pax out of his car seat so he could comfort him in the front seat, Adam reminded himself that wouldn't be safe. After Adam strapped in the two girls, he took his spot in the passenger seat, and off they went. His hand shook until he wrapped it against his belly to hide it from Karla. He wasn't sure if his body's response was from the current situation or whatever the hell he'd witnessed in the past. He had no memory of any incident with a kid and scissors.

The hospital was eight minutes away. Halfway there, he reminded Pax once more to keep pressure on his wound. The kid seemed intent on showing his sisters how strong and brave he was. At the reception window in no time, he let Karla continue to take charge explaining the situation while he held Pax in his arms and told the girls not to let go of his shirt.

Fortunately, the nursing staff allowed them all to go back with Pax, as long as they didn't become disruptive. His warning to the girls that he'd take them outside if they didn't remain quiet seemed to do the trick.

The nurse cleaned up the wound, teasing Pax so that he hardly noticed the sting. "Seems to have stopped bleeding."

"That's a relief," Karla said.

"The doctor will be here soon."

Thirty minutes later, the curtain was drawn back, and a man in a white coat entered. He looked from Pax to the girls, his eyes opening wider.

"Triplets?"

"Yes," Karla responded. "Our son has a cut at his temple that might need stitches."

"Let me have a look."

The doctor evaluated the boy. "I don't think stitches will be necessary, unless you're worried about him having a small scar. In which case, I can refer you to a plastic surgeon."

Karla glanced at Adam with a question in her eyes, but he shrugged. "It will give him bragging rights when he's older." And he could make up a much better story than that his sister cut him while trying to trim his hair.

She rolled her eyes, but smiled as she turned her attention back to the doctor. "If you think it's merely cosmetic, then I don't think we need to take that step."

"Totally cosmetic." The doctor patted Pax on the knee. "Okay then, I'll have the nurse bandage him up with Steri-Strips to keep the gash closed until it heals."

Adam didn't know what he'd have done without Karla handling this situation. Blood in combat was one thing, but maybe when it hit closer to home...

"Hang tight until the nurse returns, then we'll have you all out of here in no time." To Pax, he added, "Try not to run into any more scissors, buddy."

"I be good!"

"Hopefully, your sisters will too," Karla said, glaring at Rori as if she already knew which one had been the culprit.

"I don't know how they got the scissors out of the child-lock drawer, but we're going to store them a lot higher next time," Adam assured the doctor before he walked out of the room.

If his kids or Karla had to be rushed to the hospital again anytime soon, it would kill Adam. His job was to keep them safe.

I fucked up.

* * *

Karla

That escapade had taken ninety minutes out of their day, but at least Pax would be okay. Karla had let Savannah and Damián know what was going on and asked if they could come over about thirty minutes later than planned. She wanted time to get the kids settled in before working on dinner.

"See my butterfly dambaid, Mommy?"

"Yes, sweetheart. Your bandage is quite impressive, and you were such a brave little boy."

Pax puffed out his chest. "*Big*, brave boy!"

"Yes, you are." Karla kissed him on the cheek before he scampered upstairs with his sisters. "Do not touch anything sharp or pointy until we get up there to put everything away!" she shouted as they ran out of sight.

Adam came up behind her and wrapped his arm around her waist, pulling her against his body. His hand brushed her cheek as he tucked her hair behind her ear and kissed her neck. "How'd you stay so calm, Kitten?"

"I needed to." She didn't know what had incapacitated Adam, probably a flashback to some horror in his past, but thankfully she'd been there when her family had needed her to take charge.

Karla supposed growing up with Ian had given her an advantage in a medical crisis. She'd learned early on that head wounds bled more than injuries to other parts of the body. Or perhaps her mother's calm demeanor in a crisis had rubbed off on her.

Memories of Mom tending to Ian's many cuts, scrapes, and broken bones were quickly replaced with one of Mom treating the wounds Adam had received while fighting off the three guys at the Chicago bus station as he tried to protect teenage runaway Karla. She had only been allowed to admire his gorgeous chest before Mom sent her off on an errand rather than allow her to see the old scars and new injuries on his back.

But all had been revealed to her when they had reconnected years later. Ian's childhood wounds were nothing compared to what her husband had been through.

"Do you want to take care of the scissors or me?" Karla asked.

"If you could, I need to check on something real quick in the office."

"Go!"

She shoved him in the direction of the door and made her way up the stairs. Her lapse in judgment and becoming so lost in her work that she hadn't noticed they'd woken up, made her feel it was her responsibility to take care of this. Songwriting could wait. She needed to make sure her babies all grew to adulthood.

Or work out a better schedule so that she and Adam would not both be working at the same time. Juggling so many things at once was taking a toll, and there were few times anymore to refill the well.

The kids were playing in their room, so she quickly put the scissors on the top shelf of the linen closet and joined them to see what they were up to. She could prepare the rest of dinner while chatting with Savannah after they arrived while the dads watched the kids. Right now, they were her top priority, as they should be.

Pax sat next to a crying Rori on the floor. He had his arm around her, patting her just as Karla might do to comfort one of them. That Rori regretted the decision she'd made earlier was obvious, but seeing that Pax wanted to assuage her guilt warmed Karla's heart.

I could use a little of that myself right about now.

"Can I see your owie?" Rori asked Pax.

Pax reached for the bandage at his temple. Before he ripped it off to oblige his sister, Karla stepped into the room. "Pax, honey, let's not take our bandage off until the doctor says it's time."

He nodded, and the two of them scooted over to the pile of trucks and cars they loved to play with. Kate came over to the two of them to give them a hug, then returned to stack her blocks without a concern in the world. The three had an amazing bond that only grew stronger every day.

The ringing of the doorbell broke Karla out of her musings.

"They're here!" All three shouted as they jumped up and headed down the stairs. In hot pursuit, Karla passed Adam's closed door and called out, "I've got it, Adam!" She hoped he wouldn't remain barricaded inside too long, but he'd lost some work time this afternoon and probably needed to catch up.

Karla checked through the peephole and, as expected, found the four Orlandos on the porch, smiling. Opening the door, she stepped aside. "Come in, come in!"

Before greetings had been exchanged, Savannah hunkered down in front of Pax and asked, "How's your boo-boo?"

"Rori cut me. Now I have a special dambaid for big boys!" He turned his head so everyone could see his badge of courage.

Tomorrow, Karla needed to have a stern talk with all three about the dangers of playing with sharp things intended only for grownups. But tonight, she wanted to relish every minute with her family and their friends.

"Grammy Karla," Marisol said, "I made this for you! You wear it on your wrist."

The little girl held out a red and black friendship bracelet. "I love it, sweetie!" Karla held out her arm, and Marisol put it on her wrist. "Thank you so much, Marisol!" She gave the ten-year-old a hug and a kiss.

Kate moved in for a closer look, enthralled with the bracelet. They would probably be making jewelry together soon. Kate and Marisol had a special bond, although Marisol was good with all the kids. Karla couldn't wait until she was a teenager and old enough to babysit.

Savannah smiled as she approached and kissed Karla on the cheek before whispering, "Mari's into rope and string, just like her Grampa and Grammy."

Karla grinned. "Adam has been teaching her some special knots using the embroidery floss she never leaves home without."

"Those two crack me up when they get into an intense session with their knots," Damián said with a grin.

I just wish he'd start using some of those knots on me again!

Damián came closer with J.D. close beside him and kissed Karla's cheek too. She gave him a quick hug before hunkering down to their little boy's level. "What's that you have, J.D.?"

"'Piderman!" He held out his latest action figure to show her.

"Cool!" Rori and Pax admired his new toy, but Kate showed no interest.

"C'mon! Let's play!" Rori, always the ringleader, waved J.D. and Pax toward the play area off the kitchen. Kate and Marisol followed slowly behind them, engrossed in talk about making bracelets.

"You okay, Karla?' Savannah asked. "Pax's accident had to have freaked you out."

Karla waved away Savannah's worry. "Pax and I took it in stride." Should she mention Adam's episode? It might not hurt. With the kids out of earshot, she said in a low voice, "Adam didn't handle the sight of blood very well."

"God forbid J.D. or Mari get hurt," Savannah commiserated. "It's different when it's one of your kids. But there could be some PTSD issues too."

Karla didn't know how severe his combat traumas were, but she remembered the night when he had a night terror that sent him sailing over her hugely pregnant body without even touching her only to land on the floor ready to do battle with some unseen force. He'd refused to sleep with her much after that until after she'd recovered from her own post-birthing trauma.

Having gone through combat hell himself, Damián asked, "Should I talk with him about it?"

Damián might be able to help Adam process today's events better than anyone. "If you see an opportunity," Karla began, "it couldn't hurt."

Savannah, a social worker, suggested, "Perhaps you could find an opening to bring up how scary it must have been for him when he saw Pax bleeding. Then listen and see if he wants to say anything."

Karla loved how their friends came together to support each other at times like these.

Until Adam joined them, there wasn't much more they could do. "We'd better get to the kitchen where we can keep a closer eye on them."

She led Savannah and Damián down the hallway. After she'd served everyone a drink, Damián picked up his Dos Equis and went into the play area. Karla downed half of her glass of red wine. Maybe her nerves were more frazzled than she'd let on.

Savannah grinned and asked if she could help with anything.

"I cooked the corned beef before we headed to the hospital, but I need to add the vegetables. Won't take a minute. Already did the prep."

Hopefully, Adam would join them before too long. As if summoned by her thought, Adam ventured into the room and greeted Savannah before standing in the playroom doorway to check on the kids and to say hi to Damián.

"Now that J.D.'s old enough to get himself into trouble," Savannah began, "I probably have some emergency department runs in my future too. Fortunately, Mari is very careful with him and quite the mother hen, so any injury would probably be of his own doing while left alone too long."

After loading the cabbage, potatoes, and carrots into the pressure cooker and resealing it, Karla took a sip of wine this time.

"I still don't know where they got ahold of those shears."

"Kids are inherently curious. Wait until they come out of your bedroom carrying your vibrator during a dinner party."

"No! They didn't!"

Savannah nodded.

"Which one?"

"J.D., of course. Mari doesn't go into our bedroom without asking first." Savannah paused a moment. "Now that I think about it, maybe I'd better go back over my house again before he gets into something more dangerous than embarrassing." She shook her head and sighed. "They grow up way too fast."

"Isn't that the truth?"

Karla and Savannah enjoyed their wine a moment, and Karla wondered if she should broach this next subject, but she'd never kept anything from Savannah before. She motioned for Savannah to have a seat at the island's bar, then sat beside her and leaned closer conspiratorially.

"Savannah, how do you and Damián find time alone for yourselves?"

"Time alone?" She laughed. "What's that? It's been so long, I can't remember."

Karla's eyes opened wider. "You too?"

Savannah rolled her eyes. "It's hard to play the way we like to with a daughter who's ten going on thirty and a toddler who doesn't sleep at night."

"Tell me about it! Well, the toddler part anyway." She wondered if the triplets would be easier when they were ten, or would parenting be even harder then? "I know neither of us is comfortable with just anyone babysitting, but we need to figure something out, Savannah."

*　*　*

Savannah

At home later that evening, Savannah entered the bedroom brushing her hair. Damián laid in bed flipping through the pages of a motorcycle magazine. While he spent more time now working with Adam's security agency, Damián still supervised his Harley restoration and tried to keep up with the latest innovations.

Setting the brush on the nightstand, she stretched out beside him. Damián put the magazine aside and opened his arms for her to snuggle into.

"It was nice spending time with Adam and Karla," she began. "We don't see enough of each other—all of us together, that is."

"Yeah, everyone's so damned busy these days."

She nodded. "Karla and I talked about how hard it is to find intimacy time with kids."

"Too many inquisitive *bebés* running around." His hand moved up to cup her breast. "I bet they'll sleep well tonight, though. They were in perpetual motion playing with the other kids"

Savannah gave in to the sensation of his touching her for a few minutes and stroked his bare chest as well, but she wanted to tell him what she and Karla had cooked up tonight.

"Karla and I were talking and wondered if perhaps we might swap kids off on occasion to allow the other couple a chance for uninterrupted intimacy."

Damián's hand paused as he thought a moment. "Going from having one toddler to four might be a challenge."

"We thought if we make it late enough in the evening that they'd sleep most of the time."

He laughed. "Like J.D. and Marisol do here?"

Hmm. "Maybe we didn't think it through." She kissed him, hoping tonight might be the exception, but just as her hand wrapped round his cock, there was a soft knock at the door.

"Mama, my tummy hurts." Mari. She'd begged for a second piece of cake and now might be paying the price. Unless it was the cabbage that didn't agree with her.

Both of them sighed.

"You're absolutely right," Damián said with a sigh. "We need to figure something out."

When she started to leave the bed, he stayed her with a hand to her shoulder. "I'll see if I can calm her stomach. Then we'll pick up where we left off when I get back."

"Thank you, *mi amor.*"

She stretched out on her back after Damián left the room, but her eyelids grew heavy almost immediately.

Savannah didn't wake up until the alarm went off in the morning.

"Damián, why didn't you wake me when you came back to bed?"

"Because it was almost two hours later, and you were sound asleep."

"Is Mari okay?"

"Let's just say, she had a valid reason for saying her stomach hurt. But I cleaned up the mess."

"Oh no!" Savannah tossed off the sheet. "I'll go check on her and see if she'll feel up to going to school."

"She's sleeping now. I wouldn't worry about her unless she needs us." Before Savannah could disagree, he added, "By the way, after I got Marisol back to bed, I texted Adam. We're planning a date night as soon as we can line up babysitters."

Yes! She and Karla both needed one badly!

*   *   *

Adam

With the kids downstairs under the supervision of Patti and Victor, Adam pulled out the rope bundles he planned to use on Kitten tonight. That they'd been able to find someone to babysit on such short notice was amazing. Few people wanted to take on the triplets—much less five kids, most of them toddlers. They'd celebrated the triplets' third birthday last Saturday, so this Saturday had become their target date night. Neither Karla nor Savannah trusted many people with their children, but the kids all knew and loved Victor and Patti. Finally, the last piece of maneuvering for this night had fallen into place.

Time to focus on the beautiful woman waiting for you, Marine.

While Adam loved the beauty of decorative rope, he did not plan to focus on artistry for tonight's suspension. The two couples had no set time limit on play tonight, so Adam would make sure Karla was satisfied before turning the area over to Damián and Savannah. Both submissives had enjoyed playing at the Masters at Arms Club before family life took precedence, often watching the other couple's scene when in the public areas. Going to the club right now wasn't an option without more preparation and scheduling, but this playroom would suffice as an excellent substitute. Watching each other play would only add to their excitement this evening.

Not that any of them needed further stimulation. But he and Damián had decided Karla and Savannah would be better able to relax if one would be able to respond to any alerts from downstairs.

Get going.

Kitten, beautiful inside and out, knelt on the mat upstairs in the playroom patiently waiting for him to begin. A helluva lot more woman than Adam deserved, but every day he thanked God for taking pity on him and bringing her back into his life after she'd grown up.

And for not allowing me to fuck up my one chance—well, not too badly, anyway.

Adam unraveled the first black bundle as he joined her on the mat, kneeling behind her. "Deep breath in, Kitten." She inhaled deeply as he rubbed the loosened rope up and down her bare arms and then across her naked breasts, bringing her nipples to attention. She wore nothing but a thong, which would be easy to remove later on.

"Now, exhale even more slowly."

As she did so, Adam wrapped his arms around her and pulled her back against his chest to whisper in her ear, "Thank you for your sweet submission, Kitten."

When she had expelled the full breath just as he'd asked her to, her head lolled to the side. She'd gotten into her submissive headspace quickly, despite having such a long break between D/s scenes. Adam draped the rope loosely around her neck. He wanted her exposed and vulnerable tonight, hoping to take her where she needed to be quickly. He didn't intend to waste a moment of their precious time together.

Adam trailed his fingertips down her arms to her wrists and back up again, suddenly grabbing both of her nipples at the same time and pinching them. Her quick intake of breath made him smile. He hadn't played with her nipples while she nursed the babies, but loved having them be fair game again.

"Continue to inhale and exhale slowly, Kitten." He kept his voice soft, almost meditative.

After she completed another full breathing cycle, Adam stroked her breasts with the rope that soon would be bound around them. He let the ends dangle from her neck and moved around to stand at Karla's side, admiring her composure. He'd never grow tired of staring at her naked body. Her breasts hadn't returned to their original size post pregnancy. Both were full, their nipples dark, firm, and at the moment swollen.

He hadn't bound her tits yet. They were here for him to love on and enjoy now. He had to curb his enthusiasm to prevent himself from rushing these special moments.

Adam cupped her left breast, bending down to kiss one nipple before rubbing his lips and teeth over it. Her giggle made him hard, as always. He bit her nipple to make it swell again. Having access to her entire body without having to worry about interruptions or areas to avoid excited him so much he didn't know where to start.

Focus. Be her fucking Dom tonight.

Grabbing the ends of the rope hanging around her neck, he pulled her head closer and kissed her while sawing the rope back and forth across her nape. When he released the tension and let her sit upright again, he trailed his fingertips down her arms, leaving a trail of gooseflesh.

Letting go of the rope again, Adam took one of the black rope bundles, loosened it, and frayed the last few inches, making it into a flogger. He slapped the strands over her tits at an ever-increasing pace, loving how the stimulation kept her nipples engorged for him.

While he could have continued torturing her tits all night, it was time to start the TK chest harness she'd be suspended from. He slowly pulled on one end of the rope he'd draped around her neck until he had the entire length in his hands. Moving behind her again, he took her wrists and rotated both arms behind her, folding them over one another at a sharp angle at her lower back until her arms were at a ninety-degree angle at the elbows.

"Don't hook your thumbs around your arms, Kitten." Adam corrected her natural tendency to do so.

"Sorry, Sir. I'm a little rusty." She quickly repositioned both hands palms outward.

"Good girl." The last thing wanted was for her to sustain an injury. "You're doing great, Kitten. I know it's been a while. I don't expect perfection, but I will look out for you and take every precaution to keep you safe."

"You always have. Thank you, Sir."

Adam moved her forearms and hands a little lower to the spot just above the rise of her ass. He couldn't resist letting his hand roam over the curve of her cheeks and giving her a little slap. Her squeak of surprise brought a smile to his face. He trailed his fingertip up the crack of her ass until he took the dangling rope and fashioned a single-column above her wrists to start the box tie.

"Tell me anytime you feel tingling or numbness, so I can make the necessary adjustments."

"I will, Sir."

Adam continued working on the harness, loving the feel of the rope in his hands and with Kitten's responsive body. It had been far too long. He couldn't keep his hands off the area between her tits and neck, alternately touching her gently and applying pressure as he wrapped her upper torso. When he tightened the rope, she sighed and leaned into him.

Soon, he would have her moaning.

Moving to stand in front of her, he slipped his pointer finger between the rope and her skin to dress the wrap—making sure the rope was in a single layer and smooth all the way around, sliding his finger from the front to the back. He couldn't resist running his finger a little farther than necessary so that he could pinch one of her nipples. Her eyelids drifted shut, and she smiled, surrendering even more into the rope.

Brushing his lips along the column of her neck to her ear, he whispered, "How are you doing, Kitten?"

"Wonderful, Master Adam. Feels so good to be in your ropes once again."

"I feel the same way, Kitten."

Adam kissed her ear, tugging on its lobe with his teeth a moment before getting back to the business of blissing out his woman.

Satisfied the wrap lay flat against her skin and she was in no distress, he picked up another black rope to tie a few inches farther down her arms and below her breasts.

Adam loved to touch and tease her tits every chance he could, and this wrap allowed for any number of opportunities for him to do so. Maybe it wouldn't look so much like tit torture to her, but a functional move. He grinned as he took the nipple he'd neglected moments ago, pinched it, and lifted her breast higher to wrap the rope underneath it like an underwire. Her hiss told him she both loved and hated him stretching her nipple to the max.

Reluctantly releasing one nipple, he did the same to the other. To her credit, Kitten didn't complain or ask him to stop. She held herself straight and tall, accepting everything he did to her body with grace and submission.

Anxious to move on, Adam made quick work of the end of the rope, tying it off and dressing the wrap nice and smooth. He picked up another rope to cinch the lower wrap to the upper one on both sides.

To test her readiness for that part—and to have himself a little more fun—he pulled the rope tighter and tighter until she let out a gasp. She tried to fill her lungs, but this breathplay didn't allow her to take in much air. After a few rapid, shallow breaths, her body relaxed, and she seemed to adjust well to the pressure. It would be a lot stronger once he suspended her, but she seemed to be handling it well so far.

Adam loosened the rope a bit, though, before tying it off in the back near the single column tie to provide more stability.

Adam's heart rate ramped up.

One rope left.

While more for aesthetics than function, this last tie would not only allow him better access to play with her tits but would also help her shoulders take some of the tension away from her arms. He didn't want to add any unnecessary strain on Kitten's torso and lungs until she became used to the rope again.

Not that a little stress on her body would be a bad thing. Adam grinned as he picked up the red rope. After applying the shoulder straps to the friction at the top of the stem in the back of the harness, he pulled the rope over her shoulder and moved around to her front again. Making quick work of the design, crisscrossing the rope between her tits for a bra-like effect, he bent down to take one nipple between his lips and sucked. Kitten purred as she pushed her chest toward him. She loved having her breasts played with almost as much as he enjoyed obliging her.

Adam stepped back and applied a Munter hitch between her tits to keep the rope from slipping before completing the harness. He moved slowly to her side, his body brushing against her skin as his lips grazed her temple before he settled into place behind her. He anchored the end of the last rope to the back of the harness.

Now the fun really began, especially for his girl. She'd posed so patiently for him while he secured the chest harness. Adam circled Kitten like a panther tormenting its prey, while actually making sure everything was to his liking. He made a small adjustment to the rope over her breastbone, purely for aesthetic reasons. Every inch of rope appeared to be placed perfectly for maximum safety. Rope was the only edge play he'd engage in with her.

Pulling his focus back, he noticed his intense scrutiny had a bonus factor—heightening the awareness between her body and his. Her nipples peaked again on their own. When she opened her eyes, Kitten's nostrils flared as if scenting her mate. Soon, he'd have her suspended above the floor.

Kitten's breathing slowed as she became one with the rope. Her bare breasts rose and fell, framed by the harness around her torso, snuggly holding her upper arms to her sides.

At the same time, his breathing ramped up in anticipation. "My beautiful Kitten." He leaned in to give her a kiss while stroking her back and arms. She sighed and closed her eyes again.

"Eyes on me." He took a step back.

She opened her eyes wide as if surprised by her body's response to his command. Adam smiled. "Ka-thunk!?" He loved making her stomach drop into her pelvis as she surrendered to him.

"Yes, Sir. I've missed that feeling."

Adam kissed her cheek and whispered, "So have I, Kitten. So have I."

Ready for a little bit of a mindfuck, he picked up his rope flogger and flicked it against her outer thigh a few strokes. "Spread your legs wide open for me, Kitten."

She did so immediately, without any fear or hesitation about what he might do with the flogger next. Adam took a moment to stare at her uncovered pussy.

"So beautiful, Kitten."

His cock stirred. He wanted to bury himself deep inside her.

Not yet, Marine. You have a willing sub needing satisfaction first.

Instead of torturing her just yet, Adam used the flogger to force the blood to the surface on her bare legs, which would heighten the senses. Setting the flogger down, he tucked her left calf and heel snuggly against her thigh in preparation for tying a *futo*. That would be the second pick point he would suspend her from tonight. But for her right leg, he chose the less-restrictive single-column thigh cuff. Once again, he couldn't help but take a moment to sit back and admire her body, exposed and waiting for him. He reached for the longer bundles of red rope and stood, shook out three of them, and threw one end of each over the beam above them.

Adam anchored two more of the uplines to the points on each leg. Pulling on the torso and leg uplines, he lifted Kitten off the ground several feet. She groaned. Poor girl had been deprived of the rope for so long that she'd feel every movement intensely as her body adjusted to its new state of being. Not that he'd let her get too comfortable in any one position this early into the scene. He tied off the last upline—for now.

With her legs splayed open, he couldn't help but stare at her. While they hadn't forgone sex these past two years, everything always seemed rushed, never knowing when the kids would interrupt.

"I could look at your pussy all night, Kitten."

"Thank you, but do you think you could stare at it after you suspend me? It's been so long, Sir."

Adam flicked the flogger against her clit, making her squeal and try to close her legs. "Don't be a brat."

"I'll be good, Master Adam. You know how much I love being suspended, though. We haven't been able to since my pregnancy was deemed high risk. I've waited patiently for so long."

The plea in her voice told him he needed to get her in the air. "All right, Kitten. I'll indulge you momentarily." Adam reached for a leg upline.

Show time.

Section Two

Karla

S uddenly suspended in ropes for the first time in years, Karla's lungs constricted, and she gasped for air. Her head grew light as her body readjusted to this strange dimension she loved dearly.

"Breathe as deeply as you can for me, Kitten."

Relaxing into the rope, she did as instructed, realizing she had more lung capacity than she'd thought at first. But just barely.

"Better?"

"Yes, Sir. Thank you for reminding me…" she sucked in more air to finish her sentence, "to breathe."

The rope hugged her upper body as she swayed a foot or so above the mat. Her legs were splayed open higher off the ground.

Lord, I've missed this.

Without any way of moving her arms and very little give in her legs, Karla allowed herself to float as she sought the euphoria of flying that she loved most about being suspended.

No cares. No responsibilities. No one to take c—

A sharp sting to her nipples brought her out of her reverie. Master Adam flicked his homemade rope flogger against her breasts. He would no doubt have a lot of fun with her nipples, as well as other sensitive parts of her body, tonight.

Adam slapped the tails faster against her engorged nipples until they were hard and swollen, then he moved to her belly and lower still to her inner thighs. She braced herself just before the tails zeroed in on her bare pussy to deliver several strikes there.

Karla gasped when he connected with her clit, already swollen and aching in anticipation. A quick glance at his face showed him grinning as if excited to be here again as well. It took all the willpower she possessed not to ask him to go down on her right then, but she knew that anything she asked for would only be delayed longer. He liked for her to anticipate everything for an ungodly amount of time.

"You're so wet for me, Kitten."

Damn straight I am!

"Only for you, Sir."

"How's your chest harness feel?"

"Feels like a bear hug from you."

He smiled before going around behind her and flicking the flogger against her ass cheeks until they burned. Without explanation of what he planned to do, Karla felt a tug to the rope on her left leg seconds before he yanked the upline hard and upended her.

Augh!

Her frustrated groan had been loud enough for him to hear, because Master Adam chuckled. The shift in position threw off her equilibrium and forced her body to contort in a different way. Karla tried to fill her lungs with air, but the added pressure of the harness made it impossible to do more than catch short breaths.

Her hair hung loose below her, the tips brushing the mat. It hadn't taken long for her body to settle into that original position. Being suspended this way, the harness automatically added pressure to her lungs and body, but each time he readjusted her position, her body screamed its displeasure.

He'd begun introducing breathplay into their bedroom scenes recently, perhaps preparing her for tonight but nothing quite matched the pressure against her lungs and ribs the way being suspended did. In making the ties on her chest harness tighter, he'd taken her to that place of breathlessness immediately. Or perhaps she simply felt it more acutely after such a long absence.

The lack of oxygen allowed her mind to drift into blissful—

"How are you doing, Kitten?"

Pulled back into the scene, she sighed. "I'm getting comfortable in the rope again, Sir."

"Hmm. We'll have to do something about that."

Apparently, *comfortable* was not his intention for this suspension. Master Adam never wanted her floating away from her body until *he* was ready.

Not that she intended to complain. She'd simply have to adapt more quickly to each new position if she wanted to reach that euphoric state she loved.

Master Adam's legs and boots moved into her field of vision. If she were a little higher, she could give him a blowjob. The lack of control while in this position always made it more stimulating for her too.

Instead of opening his fly, though, he pressed his hand against her sternum and pushed her higher. She couldn't help but groan again as her body shifted. Only this time, Karla discovered that her right leg, which only had a thigh cuff on it, could now touch the mat. Well, at least her toes could. Karla giggled, but before giving herself away, she suppressed her glee. While he was busy tying her off in this new position, she used this lapse on his part as a chance to relieve some of the pressure on her upper body.

Master Adam stepped back to admire and assess his work. Karla held her breath. Surely, he'd catch on. Instead, he leaned down, fisted her hair, and pulled her head back. Hunkered down next to her, he grinned. "Doing okay now, Kitten?"

She almost batted her eyelashes at him in bratty fashion, but decided the fewer clues she gave that her predicament was much less strained than he wanted at the moment, the better.

"Fine, Sir. Thank you for asking."

Master Adam's smile grew wider, quite pleased with himself.

No doubt, he'd merely give her body time to settle for another minute or so before repositioning her. He released her hair and walked out of her line of sight. Karla tensed, waiting for him to notice.

"How did this become a partial suspension again?"

Busted!

He'd fix that soon enough. Untying one of the uplines, he lifted her left leg as high as it could possibly go, straining her thigh and groin muscles the most. Karla whimpered at the shift in position, but still dug the toes of her right foot into the mat as if she could grip hard enough to keep him from moving that leg.

"I'm not lifting this toe," Karla ground out between her teeth. "It's all I have!"

"Kitten, that's not for you to decide, now, is it?" Even though only her toes touched the mat, it kept him from fully suspending her and giving him total control. Of course, Master Adam would fix that soon enough.

And he did, yanking on the upline attached to her thigh cuff and upending her again.

Damn, that hurt!

But I won't give him the satisfaction of groaning again.

Master Adam now dominated her every move and sensation. Her mind warred with wanting to be under his thumb and wanting to take back control. She hadn't been in a position to submit to him in a while, and the desire to please him won out—this time.

Would she ever be one to simply submit to him without this internal struggle? Was it her being a brat, or did she have switch tendencies? After all, she'd tied the man to a bed once.

Analyze it later.

After securing the loose end of the rope, Master Adam moved to her other side to assess the current situation. In this new position, however, her right foot remained unrestrained. She tried stretching it out, but that didn't give her any satisfaction, so she bent her knee and pulled her foot closer to her butt. Unlike the toe-hold she'd had with the mat minutes ago, though, this lack of restriction confounded her.

As if picking up on her predicament, Master Adam took her free foot and bent it back and forth as if cranking a pump. "Not sure what to do with this bit of freedom, are you, Kitten?" He liked messing with her head like that, so he'd probably left her foot loose for that reason.

"No, Sir."

Just tie the damned thing down!

He chuckled as if he'd heard her demanding thought but soon tied the offending leg from her calf to her ankle before he moved on. Standing behind her, Master Adam pulled the rope attached to her right ankle toward him then higher, before he secured the rope.

"Oh Lord!" The contortion her body was in had her feeling muscles she'd ignored for years.

"Like that, Kitten?"

"I'm not sure *like* is the right word, Sir."

Master Adam chuckled. "Now that you mention it, that's not my goal either, even though tonight will eventually be all about your release and pleasure."

Somehow I doubt that.

At least not in the short-term. But the snugness of the rope, the presence of her Dom taking care of her most basic needs, and the freedom she'd always found being suspended soon worked together to provide her again with relief from the stresses of motherhood.

Don't think about your babies right now.

Ugh. Easier said than done.

She'd almost forgotten about Savannah and Damián watching from across the room, too, because they were so quiet. Savannah had offered to take videos and photos of their time playing, because she'd have her phone out anyway watching for any notifications from downstairs that there was a problem. Karla couldn't wait to see the images. Sometimes it was hard to know what was going on from her limited scope.

Once again, thoughts of the kids sleeping downstairs filtered into her head. It was so hard for her to let go—

Master Adam smacked her on the butt, whether because he knew her mind wasn't where it should be or for taking advantage of the slip-up in the suspension earlier, she didn't know.

"Focus on the rope, Kitten. Nothing else."

Gah.

How he could read her body so well never ceased to amaze her, but she smiled. "Yes, Master Adam."

Block out all stray thoughts! Surrender!

She'd had her short mental break and now prepared herself to continue. The feel of the rope and his magical hands as he readjusted uplines and repositioned her body every few minutes both mesmerized and distracted her. Karla took as deep a breath as possible and let it out slowly, releasing all tension from her body.

"That's my good girl."

Warmth spread throughout her body at hearing his praise.

Master Adam lowered her left leg so that once again her pussy was splayed open for him to play with. He nibbled on her inner thigh, moving closer to her core before he veered off course to her other thigh, kissing the places where the rope didn't cover her skin.

Just when she thought she'd have to scream out for him to stop teasing her, he cupped her butt and blew gently on her pussy.

Oh please! Yes!

"You smell so good, Kitten." Before she could respond, he lowered his lips to kiss her shaved mound, nibbling at her labia before releasing her butt and taking both hands to open her lower lips wide. He blew onto her clit again. She tried moving her pelvis closer to his tongue, but the way she'd been suspended, she couldn't move enough to make any difference. His tongue lapped up her juices until he pushed one finger inside her.

"Oh!"

She felt the vibration of his chuckle against her pussy.

More, Sir! Don't leave me hanging.

Poor choice of words, because hanging she would continue to do for a while longer. At last, his tongue flicked against clit as he rammed a second finger inside her.

"Yes! Please, Sir, I need to come."

He stopped all movement. *Shit.* She'd blown it.

"Is that how my kitten asks her Dom for an orgasm?"

"No, Sir, but you're driving me to distraction with your mouth and fingers. I couldn't help myself."

His laughter told her he wasn't upset with her in the least. In her most innocent tone, she asked, "Um, so, please, Sir, may I come?"

"Hmm. How long should I make you wait after that lapse in protocol?"

Please, Sir! Don't do that!

"Thirty seconds sounds like a good punishment, Sir."

"We'll double it and make it a minute. I'm in a lenient mood because it's been a while since you've submitted to me. But I'm only forgiving this one transgression."

That he only counted this as her first time being disobedient made her smile. She thought he'd have added the partial suspension one as well.

While waiting for the clock to run out, Master Adam wasn't idle. He teased her to the edge of another orgasm with his tongue and fingers, but she maintained her discipline much better this time.

Finally, his tongue lapped at her juices again, and he moved the natural lubricant from her pussy to her clit. Karla prepared herself to come. His expert ministrations heightened her emotions as the sensations roiled through her.

She waited...and waited...for him to tell her she could come. He'd promised, after all. Just before she nearly lost her composure again, he pulled away.

Noooo!

"Kitten, come for me now."

"Yes, Sir!" His tongue flicked against her clit as his fingers played with her pussy. So close. When his knuckle teased her butthole, she screamed out as she exploded for him.

Before she had time to process the mind-blowing orgasm and while her body throbbed with intense sensations, his mouth left her. With her eyes closed, relishing the remnants of heaven, suddenly her head lowered abruptly as she screamed out again. The sensory overload only heightened her experience.

Surrendering to the rope and Master Adam's hands, Karla floated away.

*   *   *

Karla

A warm hand supported her back while a thumb flicked at her sensitive nipple. Karla opened her eyes to find herself sitting on Master Adam's lap in the playroom. Disoriented, she glanced across the room to see that Damián had Savannah strapped to the spanking bench, her ass already as red as a strawberry.

She had no clue how long she'd been in subspace, but Karla snuggled against Master Adam's warm chest. "That was incredible," she whispered so as not to disturb the couple playing across the room. Her voice sounded husky, mellow.

"Glad you liked it, Kitten," Adam whispered. "I enjoyed the hell out of you myself." He handed her a bottle of water. "Drink this."

As she did so, his hand moved away from her nipple, down across her abdomen, and toward her pussy. "Spread your legs."

Karla complied immediately, letting her left foot drop to the floor to give him all the access he wanted. She turned her face toward him, and he kissed her, his tongue entering her mouth as his thumb drew lazy circles around her sensitive clit. Even though she remembered coming at least once before her total surrender, she wasn't sure how long she could hold out before this next one.

He pulled away and whispered, "You're going to come for me again, Kitten."

At least I don't have to beg this time.

"But you aren't going to make a sound when you do. We don't want to interrupt their scene."

Never one for quiet orgasms, even though they'd been practicing the technique of silent ones for a while now so as not to wake up the babies sleeping across the hall, she intended to do her damnedest.

"I'll try my best."

He stopped stroking her. "You *will* come silently, or you won't come at all."

Okay, if you put it that way.

"Yes, Sir. I *am* going to come silently."

Master Adam grinned. "I thought you might see things my way." He rammed three fingers inside her without preparation or warning, and it was all she could do not to cry out at how wonderfully full she felt. Instead, she pressed her lips together tightly and closed her eyes.

"No, Kitten. Eyes on me. I want you to watch their scene while I get you off on it—albeit quietly."

Karla didn't need any encouragement to get off, although watching someone enduring some serious pain had always been a turn-off for her. However, she wanted—no, needed—this orgasm. Turning her head back to where the other couple played across the room, she watched. Adam kept his fingers firmly inside her but didn't move them. And his thumb had stopped rubbing her clit. Apparently, he intended for her to get off on the scene before them without much stimulation from him.

Damián stroked Savannah's red ass, and she moaned. For those two, a spanking bench was rather tame, so she wondered what else Damián had planned for Savannah and how long they'd been in their scene already. She'd lost all sense of time.

Circling around her, holding some kind of chain-mail flogger—*dear Lord!*—Damián zeroed in on her breasts placed on either side of the narrow padded seat her chest rested on. Her knees rested on kneelers on either side, leaving her ass and pelvic area exposed off the end of the bench. Damián pinched her nipples, then stepped back and flicked the tips of the chain mail flogger against them. Savannah hissed in pain or surprise.

"Like that, Kitten?"

Her pussy must have contracted against his fingers. "Only to watch, Sir." *You'd better not try anything that painful on me!*

Damián landed additional whacks of the metal falls against her ass. Savannah could handle a bullwhip, but Karla had no clue if she'd experienced this type of flogger before. Karla had never seen one. When he landed those evil tails against her reddened ass, Karla clenched against Adam's fingers again. Savannah had a high pain tolerance, but even she began to cry out and squirm after he'd landed several strikes in a row, alternating between her nipples and ass. She'd only weaned J.D. a few weeks ago, so her nipples might be the most sensitive of the two areas.

Karla thrust her hips against Adam's hand, pulled away, then pushed against him once more. She wished she had his cock inside her but had no doubt they'd make love once they returned to their bedroom for the night.

Unless Adam wasn't finished with her up here tonight. Would he have sex with her in front of Damián and Savannah?

Karla stiffened, not sure she was ready for that.

"What's the matter, Kitten?"

Damián rained the flogger's tails against Savannah's ass relentlessly, but her moans neared orgasmic tones as she accepted each stroke.

"I, um, don't think I'd like having that thing used on me."

When Damián flicked it directly against her exposed clit out of the blue, Savannah screamed, "Oh, my God!"

Karla's pussy clenched around Adam's fingers.

"I didn't know you got off on pain, Kitten" Adam whispered.

"Neither did I. I mean, I don't. Unless I'm watching it happening to someone else, I suppose." No way did she want Adam to inflict that level of pain on her.

Do I?

His body shook in a silent chuckle as they continued trying to keep from intruding, not that Savannah or Damián would probably have noticed the two of them. They were too deep into their scene. Still, Karla vowed to remain quiet.

When would Adam let her come? Had he and Damián discuss their plans ahead of time with each other? What was he waiting for?

"Sir!" Savannah cried out. "Please!" Karla wasn't certain if she was pleading for him to stop or to give her something more.

A grin spread over Damián's face, and he started to unbutton the flap of his leathers to pull out his erection. Karla glanced away, not wanting to watch them having sex. Of course, they must have watched Adam go down on her earlier.

"Did I tell you to stop watching them?" Adam pulled his fingers out of her pussy and moved his hand away.

Seriously? They'd never watched other couples do that before. At the Masters at Arms Club, all sexual activity happened in private rooms, at least it had when Adam, Damián, and Marc owned the place. She assumed that was still true under Mistress Grant's leadership.

"No, Sir. I'm sorry." Reluctantly, she forced her gaze back to the couple across the room. Adam shoved his fingers inside her again, then stilled. She pleaded silently for him to stroke her clit and let her get off, but of course, she couldn't ask or he'd never deliver.

She was entitled to one slip, but not two in the same night.

However, Savannah and Damián's protocols must be different than hers and Adam's because she appeared to be begging for it.

In the position Damián had strapped Savannah down, he could enter her mouth, pussy, or ass. Karla waited, wondering which he'd choose. Any of the three would be as hot as hell.

I didn't know I had a voyeur streak in me.

But her Dom obviously did. He seemed to know everything about her, always pushing her to broaden her horizons.

Damián moved around to Savannah's head, and without a word, he thrust his cock inside her mouth and held it there. *Jesus!* She must have been prepared and waiting for him, because there seemed to be no resistance, not even a gag reflex. As Damián withdrew and reentered her continually, Karla became wetter.

She squirmed in Master Adam's lap, hoping he would take the hint and play with *her* again, but he didn't make a move.

"Deep breath through your nose, *savita.*"

When she complied, Damián grabbed Savannah's head with both hands and pushed his cock's full length even farther down her throat and held it there once again. He closed his eyes, clearly enjoying himself. She didn't know how Savannah was taking it. Damián looked as though he was close to coming.

However, he pulled out instead, patted her on the top of her head, and bent down to kiss her, praising her for deep throating him. Damián stepped back and prepared himself with a condom. Apparently, they were trying not to have more kids, either. When he returned to her raw butt cheeks, he pushed three fingers inside her pussy.

"Yes, Sir! Please! I need you!" Her voice sounded raspy, raw, and sexy as hell. Karla had never perfected deep throating, although she did enjoy sucking on Master Adam's cock. Should she ask Savannah for tips, or would YouTube allow such videos to educate her? She'd learned a lot from the site already. But she wanted to please Adam in that way too.

Damián pulled out his fingers and immediately drove his cock to the hilt inside her pussy. He began thrusting in and out as he held onto her sore hips, as if she could go anywhere. Karla panted as Savannah's moans grew more desperate. Would Master Adam let her come when Savannah did?

Please, Sir. Let me come too!

Unfortunately, he remained perfectly still as he watched the other couple, but she felt his hard cock pressing against her butt. He had to be purposefully denying her this much-needed release.

Ugh! The man could be so infuriating sometimes.

"Come for me, *savita*." Damián reached beneath her, most likely to play with her clit, and their cries of ecstasy elicited a moan from Karla too.

"Like that, do you, Kitten?"

"Yes, Sir." She ground out the words, ticked off that he wasn't letting her come too. "I had no idea I would. I know what would make it even better."

He merely chuckled, the bastard. As always, he knew what she'd like even before she did.

"And what might that be, Kitten?" Karla glared at him, and he raised his eyebrows, then grinned. "Jealous, Kitten?"

She met his gaze. "Well, I'm definitely jealous of her orgasm!" Karla realized too late that she hadn't whispered that time, but glancing across the room, she saw that the other couple was so deep in their own pleasure they didn't seem to notice.

Master Adam's thumb finally rubbed against her clit as his fingers went deeper inside her in search of her G-spot. She threw her head back in sweet abandon as the delicious waves washed through her. Leaning her back against the arm of the loveseat, he leaned down and took her left nipple into his mouth, chomping down hard until she almost moaned again, but she fought to stay as quiet as she could out of respect for the other couple in the playroom. Despite her best efforts, her panting and moaning grew louder as she fought to crest with this orgasm.

Fortunately, he didn't chastise her, but also hadn't given her permission to come. Sir liked to be in control of the exact moment she exploded, whether they were engaging in vanilla sex or hot-as-sin kink. His mouth released her sore nipple. "Make all the noise you want when I give you permission to come, Kitten. Damián and Savannah are wrapping things up."

She'd lost track of them altogether in the past few moments.

"Keep your eyes on me, Kitten. I want to watch your face as you come."

Karla met his gaze without blinking. He smiled. "Come for me, Kitten. Now."

A few more strokes on her swollen bundle of nerves was all it took. Her pelvis bumped against his hand, and she wrapped her arms around his neck to hold on. She needed this so m—

"Yes! Yes! Oh!" The explosion rocked her world as she screamed, "Oh Lord! I mean, Sir, I'm coming!" Her hips bucked as she rode the edge of ecstasy before tumbling over to the other side. She wished she could have lasted longer, but this one was even more intense than the first one tonight, bringing her to tears. She closed her eyes until he pinched her clit, and she remembered to look at him while at the same time trying to squirm away from his hand. His thumb and finger continued to torment her clit; Master Adam liked adding a bit of torture after she came.

When he'd apparently had enough, thankfully, he wrapped a blanket around her and pushed her head onto his shoulder. "Rest a bit while we wait for Damián to clean up, because I'm not finished with you yet tonight, Kitten."

Despite being completely sated at the moment, no way would she complain if he wanted to play more. Victor and Patti were spending the night in one of the guest rooms.

Karla felt loved, cherished. He hadn't grown tired of her at all, despite how her body had changed in the past few years. The promise in those words made her ready for more instantly. She couldn't wait for him to get off too. He had much more self-control than she did.

Assuming Savannah must be in aftercare, too, Karla focused solely on what she and her Dom had done. Adam had some of the uncoiled rope draped around his neck from when he'd taken her down from the beam. She closed her eyes, knowing he wouldn't insist she keep them open any longer.

"We're off to bed now," Damián said. Karla jerked awake to find him leading an equally serene Savannah by the hand toward the stairway.

"Good night," Adam said. "Thanks for the letting us watch."

Karla's face grew warm at Adam's words, and she averted her gaze from the other couple. How would she ever face them again without blushing after witnessing such an intimate moment between them? Of course, they'd watched her and Adam, too, although the two of them hadn't made love. Yet.

Damián chuckled. "Anytime. I think my Princess Slut is discovering that she likes watching *and* being on display. Made her hotter than a firecracker all night."

Karla ventured a glance at them. A blush crept up Savannah's neck to her cheeks, but she smiled at her Dom.

Karla had no idea! The two girls definitely had a lot to talk about the next time they could find time away from their husbands and kids.

*　*　*

Adam

Tonight, he and Damián had given both their wives a new kink to add to the list of what they each enjoyed. Next time, he and Karla might try having sex in front of the younger couple. Adam could still show Damián a trick or two for getting his wife off, not that he was lacking in any way.

Thank goodness Karla and Savannah had brought up this idea. Clearly, they'd missed having time for kink, too, not to mention time away from the kids. The two couples hadn't played at the Masters at Arms Club in longer than Adam could remember, but he might make it a monthly priority now, even if they couldn't all go together and had to alternate babysitting duties.

They would rekindle their kink with baby steps, though, playing more at home than they had been lately.

Victor and Patti must be sound asleep already in the room down the hall. Damián and Savannah had the room across the hall from Karla's studio. He and Karla should have more date night left, if Karla was up to it. He hadn't removed her chest harness yet, except for freeing her arms. The ropes had been removed from her legs as well, but he had plenty of rope in the bedroom to bind her again.

"Tired, Kitten?" Adam asked when they were alone in their bedroom as he removed his boots and leathers until he was naked too.

"Not at all, Sir. More like…mellow." Her sweet, submissive smile made him hard. "And I believe we have some unfinished business, Sir."

She stepped closer, and her fingertip drew teasing circles high on his bare thigh, working its way closer and closer to his balls, but falling short. His cock bobbed in anticipation.

Adam glanced across the room at the rope hammock chair on its tripod frame, and a slow smile spread across his face. *Perfect.*

But first, a little more old-fashioned torture for his kitten. Karla's exposed nipples begged for his attention. He leaned in as if to kiss one, but bit it gently instead. Her gasp pleased him. He'd missed those sounds, but she hadn't disappointed him tonight.

Adam went to the drawer beside his bed and pulled out some of the thin rope he'd been using to teach Marisol how to tie knots for her bracelets. Not as thin as the embroidery floss she used on the final product, but perfect for what he had in mind now.

He took the twenty-four-inch strand of red rope by both ends, pulled it taut, and rubbed it up and down over her nipples until both were swollen and ready for him. He'd let her nips shrink a little bit before tying them, but this would help him gauge the tightness of the nooses. Her body had changed since the babies—and was sexier than ever to him.

Pathetic that he'd gone so long without indulging in one of his favorite kinks.

Adam fashioned one noose about six inches from the end of the rope and another equal distance from the other end. Memories of the first time he'd put her nips into nooses flooded back.

Good times.

When her nipples relaxed a little, he tied the first noose just tight enough to stay on. Keeping it there wouldn't be a problem in a few minutes, though.

Letting the end of that string dangle, Adam returned to his nightstand drawer and pulled out several fishing weights. They'd been in there a long while for this purpose without ever having been used. Such a pity. He added several pea-sized weights to the loose end of the string. After gauging the weight, he added a fourth one before forming a noose around her other nip.

Focusing on her face, he pulled his hand back and let go of the weights all at once. Karla's eyes burst open along with her mouth, and she squeaked out a pain-filled sound.

Dear lord, I love that sound.

"How does that feel, Kitten?"

Already adjusting to the pressure, she smiled. "Nice. Snug."

He bit back a grin, wondering if she'd feel the same way about them in a few minutes. Once again, Adam returned to his nightstand drawer—which had become a makeshift adult-toy box—

and pulled out a dragon's tail. "Straighten your back and place your hands on the rise of your ass, palms outward."

Karla assumed the position without hesitation and presented herself to him beautifully. *So pretty.* Adam tugged the thin rope upward, lifting both nipples just to the edge of pain. Her hiss told him when she'd reached her limit and then he pulled a little higher.

Augh!

Her groan as her eyes shut tight made him smile. She wasn't a pain slut, but he so enjoyed pushing her to her limits, if only briefly.

"Eyes on me, Kitten."

After she'd complied, with his pointer finger still hooked around the string pulling her behind him, Adam walked her across the room toward the hammock chair. What else could she do but follow unless she wanted to add more torture to her nipples?

Stopping a yard or so away from the frame, he released the weights to another groan, but she kept her focus on his face. Adam stepped back and lifted the dragon's tail to begin flicking the tail against her swollen nips, alternating from one to the other as he watched them double in size. Her eyes opened wider, but she didn't complain about how tight or sore they were becoming.

"That's my good girl."

When he sped up the pace, Kitten shifted her weight from one leg to the other as if that would help redistribute the discomfort.

"Remain still, Kitten, or this will get worse for you."

"Yes, Sir." She closed her eyes to absorb the pain.

"Eyes on me," he reminded her sharply.

She met his gaze with a delightful mix of annoyance and trust that nearly gutted him. How'd he get so lucky?

Seeing that her nips probably were at their maximum size, he leaned in and bit one again, only harder this time than earlier.

Kitten screamed, "Oh!" Quickly remembering they weren't alone in the house, she added, "Sorry, Sir. This was so intense that I forgot my discipline."

Adam bit the other even harder and held on longer, but she maintained her composure this time.

He stood upright and stroked her cheek. "That's my girl."

Once again, he flicked the tail of the tiny-but-mighty whip against her areolas and the fleshy part of her breasts until they were nice and red.

"Spread your legs." She did so somewhat tentatively. "Wider." When he tapped the inside of her left foot with his own, she stretched them even farther apart. "That's good." No doubt she feared he'd use the implement as hard on her most sensitive area as he had on her tits. Adam grinned.

Her pussy exposed to him now, he decided to tease his way upward with the flogger, focusing on the insides of her thighs. When she closed her eyes and her head lolled a bit, he knew just how to get her to focus on him again without saying a word.

Adam flicked the dragon's tail upward against her clit.

"Jesus!" Her eyes shot open, and she glared at him for spoiling her good feeling.

Adam grinned and flicked it again on the same spot. "You will keep your eyes open now, won't you, Kitten?"

"Yes, Sir."

To her credit, she hadn't moved out of the position he'd put her in. "You're doing great in every other way tonight, Kitten. We'll have to keep working on you keeping your eyes open when told to, though." He stepped closer and kissed her far too briefly on the lips. Later, he'd give those lips the attention they deserved. "Thank you for surrendering your body to me tonight."

At his praise, she relaxed again and smiled. And she kept her eyes on him this time. "I'd forgotten how much I loved this."

Adam would do whatever he could to make sure she never again spoke words of regret about their playtime.

Soon, though, she wouldn't be able to speak words of any kind.

* * *

Karla

Master Adam continued to alternate flicking the dragon's tail against her nipples and her clit, eventually lulling her into a delicious mellowness she'd needed for so long. She let the sensations envelop her.

Without warning, Master Adam yanked her head back by a fistful of her hair, and she nearly came. God, how she loved having him pull her hair. Too late, though, she realized she'd closed her eyes again.

Darn it, he made me feel so good; how could I not enjoy it that way?

Master Adam stepped away to remove the hammock chair from the curved steel frame, and Karla wrinkled her brow wondering why. Taking the rope he had hanging from his neck, he tossed it over her head and around her lower back, reeling her in until she stood next to him and the now-bare tripod. Moving the rope higher, he sawed it back and forth against the bare part of her shoulders, then let one end go and draped it around his neck again.

"Turn around, Kitten."

She did as instructed, presenting him with her back. Retrieving her yoga mat from the corner, he opened it at her feet under the tripod. "Sit on the mat with your legs open, feet flat on the floor, and knees bent as sharply as possible."

Assuming the position as best she could to the point where she feared she might topple backward. He pushed her head and upper body forward between her open legs.

That's better. I think.

Master Adam had never put her in this position before, so she grew anxious as she waited to see what would come next. He went to the closet to get his rope bag. So he'd be tying her up again.

Retrieving a bundle of red rope, he unwrapped and wound it

several times around her leg just above her right knee before securing one end and tugging the remainder of the rope around her back.

"Take three slow, deep breaths."

After she'd completed the third, Master Adam pressed down on her back several times as he adjusted the rope through what she supposed were loops in her harness. Despite Karla's thinking she couldn't bend any closer to the floor, he pushed against her back once again. Soon, his deft fingers tied her other leg in similar fashion. The position pushed her diaphragm, making it more difficult to take a deep breath. She tested the bonds but couldn't close her legs even a tiny fraction of an inch.

The position held lots of possibilities for intimate touching and even sex, though. She couldn't wait for him to continue—but didn't have to.

Grabbing her by the hair again, Master Adam pulled her into an upright, seated position again.

Ka-thunk!

Taking her arms, he crossed them over and between her breasts and attached them to her chest harness with a short rope. Totally immobile, Karla waited for her Dom to do whatever he wanted with her.

"Breathe in as deeply as you can." She did so, and he nodded, apparently satisfied that she wouldn't pass out from a lack of oxygen. Now that she was upright again, though, she could breathe more easily. "Continue to breathe deeply for me."

His reminding her to breathe usually came before he deprived her of full breaths during a suspension scene. Karla stared at the tripod frame again, considering alternate uses for it. She wouldn't be lifted far off the floor, but the idea intrigued her as to the possibilities of being in this exposed and vulnerable position. Had he bought this chair and its frame for this purpose all along? She'd only used it to swing with her babies, but after tonight, she wouldn't be able to look at it the same way again.

Next, he took the rope that had been hanging around his neck and attached it to the back of her harness much as he'd done in the playroom earlier. So suspension would definitely be in the cards again tonight.

Thank the Lord.

After he secured the rope, he took the yoga mat and moved her entire body in between the three metal legs of the frame. Master Adam drew the loose rope through the suspension points at the back of her harness before threading the remaining rope through the hook at the highest point of the frame. She didn't worry about it being able to hold her, because she sat in the chair all the time, usually with all three toddlers piling on.

She held her breath and closed her eyes, waiting. When he didn't do anything right away, she opened one eye slightly to find him in front of her staring at her oh-so-wet pussy. The expression of worship on his face only made her wetter.

Karla smiled as Master Adam disappeared behind her again. Without warning, he pulled on the rope and hefted her body off the ground as if she were light as a feather. Gravity pulled at the weights on her nipple nooses, making them grow larger within the confines of the string. Her chest harness restricted her breathing somewhat, as expected. Bombarded with so many sensations at once, she surrendered to his will and waited for what would happen next.

Master Adam secured the rope, knelt in front of her, and taking her by the hips, pulled her pussy against his erection. After a slight shake of his head, he released her to swing slightly as he went behind her again and hefted her an inch or two higher.

He must be lining her up with his cock. This position became more promising all the time!

Once again, he knelt before her, grabbed her hips, only this time, he bent his head down to her pussy. His tongue and lips pressed against her sensitive skin and lower lips as he placed a row of nibbles and kisses from the juncture of her left leg and hip toward her clit. Unfortunately, when she expected him to lavish attention on her pussy or clit, he started down her other thigh doing the same.

Always the tease!

But eventually, he'd get to where she wanted him, probably after he'd whipped her into a frenzy of desire. Anticipation was half the fun, as he'd taught her over the years. He tugged at the nooses, reminding her of how vulnerable her tender nips were, but soon let them go. His thumbs spread open her labia, and he blew on her clit, still sensitive from the dragon's tail treatment minutes ago.

More!

When he stopped, she groaned.

"Is there something wrong, Kitten?"

Hmm. How to answer? If she told him she wanted more, he'd make her wait for it. "No, Sir. Everything's ducky."

His hand slapped her ass cheek.

"Don't be a brat."

"I'll try not to be, Sir." She smiled, knowing Master Adam expected nothing less than for her to be a brat, though. He loved it.

But he slapped her other ass cheek, too, as if for good measure.

Oh! "I mean, yes, Sir, I will do as you say."

She didn't want to have to add punishment to the session because that would only delay them both from getting what they wanted.

Master Adam tucked her clit between his lips and pulled. It took all the discipline she could muster not to cry out.

More, Sir!

Karla gave in to the intense sensations roiling throughout her body. His sucking and nibbling brought her to the brink of an orgasm, but she needed to be given permission to come. She didn't intend to beg for it unless he told her to do so.

He tugged at her nipple nooses again, and it dawned on her that those would have to come off at some point. Given how tight they were, that would not be pleasant. But at the moment, if that's what it would take for him to get off and let her come, she didn't care. She needed release, even though it hadn't been that long since her last orgasm.

Now!

Unfortunately, he kept her on the edge of coming. Just when she'd almost tumble over the cliff, he'd stop and do something else and let her relax somewhat before he brought her close to the peak again.

Please, Sir! I need this so badly!

Her silent pleas were ignored as once again his tongue flicked against her clit. Then he stood abruptly, and he picked up the dragon's tail.

Oh shit. He wouldn't!

Master Adam began flicking it against her thighs. Karla held her breath, waiting for the impact she knew would be next, but he struck at her sore nips instead. Just when the sensation brought her to the edge of coming—without him even touching her clit again— he stopped.

He pinched her nipples once more. Karla held her breath, knowing what was about to happen. Instead, Master Adam grabbed his cock. *Oh, yes!* He quickly rolled on a condom. For the past three years, he always used multiple means of birth control to avoid another pregnancy.

Don't think about babies right now, Kitty!

Fiddling again with the strings attached to her nipples, he loosened and released the noose on the left and then did the same with the right one. Just before pain radiated through her chest from the blood flow returning to her nipples, Master Adam grabbed her by the rope on the left side of her harness and swung her body slightly away from him.

She fought back a scream as the pain crashed into her nipples Closing her eyes, she felt her body being pushed back before he yanked her forward and rammed himself inside her to the hilt.

Dear Lord! So full.

Karla had needed no lubrication, and he'd known she wouldn't. The sensations bombarding her from her burning, stinging nipples to her swollen clit to Master Adam's cock driving in and out of her sent her mind into a frenzy of want and need. He pounded her rhythmically as he swung her back and forth for what seemed like forever but was probably only a few minutes.

She fought the urge to come. He hadn't given her permission yet.

Please! I'm so close, Sir!

Master Adam ground out the command, "Come with me, Kitten."

At last!

She wouldn't have been able to hold this one back much longer, no matter what diabolical punishment he devised to discipline her.

While she'd thought she would come immediately, she found it difficult to do so at the last minute. Karla tried to squeeze her knees around his waist, but couldn't budge. She wished her hand was free to stroke herself, but the way he'd restrained her arms left no room for movement there, either.

"Help me, Sir!" He reached between their bodies and rubbed her clit, finally sending her over the precipice. "Oh, Adam! Yes!"

"Fuck, yes!" he shouted as he exploded inside her.

Karla smiled. He'd been trying so hard not to use that word anymore because of the kids, but it only proved that he felt his orgasm as profoundly as she did hers.

Adam continued to plunge the full length of his cock inside her, pull out, and enter her again a few more times, but he gradually slowed his pace.

Karla opened her eyes and smiled at the look of wonder in his as he came, giving her a sense of power she rarely felt anywhere else.

What an amazing night. She couldn't wait to do it again.

Section Three

Megan

"Me next, Unca Wyder!" Pax shouted, jumping up and down as he tugged on Ryder's shirt before her husband could even put Rori back on the mounting block and pick him up.

"Again! Again!" Rori demanded, refusing to relinquish her spot on her uncle's back.

Karla, sitting at the other end of the bench on Megan and Ryder's front porch, shook her head and turned toward Megan. "Those two are going to wear Ryder out."

A pang of regret stabbed Megan, and she turned away from her sister-in-law's face. "Trust me, Karla, he's loving every minute of it." Megan's eyes stung, and she shifted her gaze toward the distance, unable to watch the scene before them.

"Aunt Megan, what's wrong?" Kate asked, patting her aunt's arm. Kate had such a big heart and always empathized with anyone who was hurting.

Megan forced a smile for the little girl. "Oh, nothing, baby girl. I just tear up when I'm super happy." She scooped up Kate and set her on her lap. "And seeing you all here at the ranch having so much fun makes Aunt Megan *very* happy!" She kissed her niece on the top of her head. Satisfied all was right with her aunt's world, Kate squirmed off her lap to chase after Hero and his grown littermates who were getting reacquainted with each other and Chance.

Karla placed her hand on Megan's forearm and squeezed it in a show of comfort. Megan had confided in Karla several years ago why she wouldn't be able to have kids.

Megan forced a smile as she turned toward her again. "On days like this, I regret my decision when I was young to stop the pain and have that hysterectomy."

"I hate that you were in so much pain to have to make a choice like that."

"If I hadn't been in such a hurry, I might have done more research and learned I could have harvested my eggs first, but…" Anger bubbled up at her physician for not asking her at the time, but she pushed it aside. Being bitter wouldn't change anything. Trying to lighten the mood, she added, "Given my low tolerance for pain, I might not have survived giving birth."

Karla waved away her words. "I forgot about the pain soon enough, although I'm not sure Adam's forgotten yet." Both of them laughed, although remembering how Karla had almost died and what it had done to Adam sobered Megan.

"Have you and Ryder thought about adopting?"

"Only in generalities. There's been so much to do here at the ranch that I don't know when we'd have time to start the process."

Karla had to laugh. "If we waited until we're ready for kids, no matter how we get them, no one would be parents. I don't think Adam would have intentionally wanted to have kids at all. He was happy to take on the role of Grampa to Marisol and thought that would be satisfying enough."

Would Adam have even married her if they hadn't accidentally gotten pregnant? Karla pushed the thought aside. No one else would put up with him, and he knew it. Not that he would have married anyone else, either, though. But he'd eventually figured it out and had come after her. Their unexpected pregnancy merely gave him the nudge he needed to pop the question.

Megan smiled. "I suppose that might be true of Ryder to some degree, as well. I think he had it hard growing up, which might factor into his reluctance too." She looked across the yard to where he played with all three triplets now. "But just look at him with his nieces and nephew. He'd be good with his own kids too. I wish I could…"

Megan's voice cracked, and Karla wrapped her arms around her. "I'm sorry, Karla. I don't know what's the matter with me today. I don't usually get like this."

"You don't have to hide anything from me, Megan." They simply held each other in silence for a minute or two before Megan pulled away.

"Some days are harder than others." Again, she tried to lighten the conversation. "But I hope you don't mind us spoiling your three. They are such a joy to have around."

"Spoil away! They don't get to see their grandparents as often as I'd like, so they need to be doted on by extended family every chance they can be. Speaking of which, do you think you and Ryder will be able to join us at the Black Hills cabin in August?"

"We're hoping to. It'll be fun if we can get our entire family together."

Patrick and Megan hadn't met Adam until they were grown, and Mrs. Gallagher had decided this year to start bringing the whole family together annually at the cabin that had been passed down in the Montague line for almost a century and a half.

"Adam and I haven't been up there since our honeymoon, and it will be the first time for the kids," Karla said.

"We still have some logistics to work out, but Luke and Cassie will be around, and Angelina's brother Matt and his bride-to-be plan on helping after their honeymoon, before Dakota starts college."

Matt and Dakota had been a great help to them earlier this year when Luke and Cassie went to Peru, but the two had a lot going on this summer planning their wedding and honeymoon.

"Great! I can't wait to fly on Patrick's new jet."

"He loves his newest toy, although I know he plans to book private charters, too, since it can accommodate twelve passengers."

"The kids are excited to fly with him in August. We're driving to Chicago next weekend for a belated birthday get-together for Adam and the triplets. They won't be able to compare that trip with the glamour of flying, but they'll be spoiled for all future trips."

"You should see if Patrick can fly you."

"No, Adam insists that we shouldn't pull him away from paying customers. He's just starting out. Besides, they're three. How much will they remember of the plane ride anyway?" Karla glanced toward the barn. "Do you think those two will ever come out of there?"

Megan laughed. "I'm not sure, but I hope you're ready for whatever he brings home this time."

Karla laughed. "Believe me, I will be. Luke does make such wonderful pieces." She cocked her head. "So, you and Ryder…"

Megan could feel the blush creeping up her neck and couldn't make eye contact. "We dabble occasionally."

"I've never noticed any special equipment in your house."

"Oh Luke is very good at disguising it as functional furniture."

"True! I'm sure you wouldn't be able to point out what we use for kink and what's used for other functions at our place, either. I can't wait to see what we're going to be adding to our collection."

Uncomfortable talking about kink involving her brother, Megan glanced toward the house. "I'd better go check on the lemon chicken and see if I can help Cassie with anything."

"I'd love to help, but I probably should round up the kids and feed them so that I can have dinner with the grownups." Karla laughed as she stood and called the triplets to come inside with her.

"Sounds like a great plan. I'm sure you've got it down to a science."

"I'm trying!"

*   *   *

Adam

A shirtless Luke Denton worked with one of his skittish mustang rescues. The thick, rough rope dangling around Luke's neck sent Adam's thoughts to what he'd come out to the corral to talk to the exceptionally patient man about. How would Luke feel about what Adam wanted to propose?

The horse rope around Luke's neck had to be as scratchy as hell, not the much softer rope he had in mind. Now that Cassie seemed to be able to tolerate being within arm's distance of Adam, something he also attributed to Luke, he wanted to try something new with their wives to expand their horizons, if you will.

Adam grinned.

His and Karla's newfound freedom now that they were playing again made the possibilities limitless. Cassie and Luke didn't have kids yet to cramp their style, but they'd find out soon enough when they did how precious time to play could become.

"Easy, Calder." Luke held out his hand to the horse, not touching it but merely getting closer. "I'm not going to hurt you, boy."

Adam became mesmerized watching Luke for the next half hour as he came closer and closer to the stallion to where he could touch the horse's back without it skittering away.

Amazing shit.

"Good boy. Now, I think that's enough for today."

Luke opened the gate and the stallion tore off into the open pasture.

"How long is it going to take to saddle that horse?" Adam asked.

"Another day or two. Later tonight, Pic and I will ride out to find him and bring him back for his next session."

"You certainly seem to have their ear when you work with

them, but I noticed Calder didn't turn his eye away from you the entire time."

Luke chuckled. "Nope. Trust takes a long time to build."

Perfect opening.

"Speaking of trust, I wanted to propose something to you and see if you're interested."

"Shoot." Luke locked the corral gate behind him and turned toward Adam.

"Karla and I have begun doing some rope play again now that we've been able to line up some babysitters, and I'd like to try something new with her in a few months after we're back up to speed. But we'll need another couple, and I wondered if you'd like to take your rigging skills to the next level and join us."

Adam explained what he had in mind, and Luke heard him out, then asked, "You sure I could get to that skill level in a couple months?"

"We'll definitely need to have some sessions where I can show you some more advanced techniques. And you won't do *any* full suspensions without me or another skilled rigger present." Adam gave him a pointed look. He didn't want him getting overly confident without supervision.

"Wouldn't dream of it."

"Work on getting Cassie used to the ties, mostly the TK chest harness and the *futomomo* ones I showed you before. We can work on some the suspension techniques when I see you again."

"I think it would be something Cassie might enjoy doing, especially if her best friend will be a part of it."

The girls had been best friends since college. In fact, the only reason Karla came to Denver four years ago—after her brother, Ian, died—was to be closer to Cassie. Thank God his kitten had shown up to audition as a singer at Adam's kink club. He didn't want to think about his life without Karla and their kids in it.

"Hey, Cassie and I have to set up a gallery exhibit in Denver next week. Maybe we could drop by then."

"Sounds perfect. Stay with us at the house. We have plenty of room. But I'm afraid my suspension equipment is still pretty basic, if we want to practice."

"Follow me." Luke led him to the smaller of the three barns, the one that held Luke's studio where he turned out some of the finest fucking kink equipment around.

Inside, Luke led him to a back corner and pointed up to the ceiling where a forged sorting hook had been inserted into the beam.

"Looks like you've already been thinking about doing some suspension work." That hook would be strong enough to hold a couple tons of weight. Overkill, but Adam appreciated the man's cautious nature when it came to rope play, assuming that's what he planned to use it for.

"This winch and pulley system has just been waiting for the right moment for me to ask you to teach me some suspension skills." Luke grinned.

Adam shook his head. "We're definitely on the same wavelength then."

"I'd love a rope-suspension tutorial from you this week, too, if you're offering one in your playroom. Cassie's been under a lot of stress lately to get ready for this show, so if she can relax enough, it'll be good for her."

"I'd be happy to, and we'll make sure Karla can provide some moral support."

"So you think something like this would work in your playroom? It's been a while since I've been up there, so I don't know what else you have."

"Honestly, it hasn't changed much since Marc lived there." Adam glanced up at the hook again. "With Karla's pregnancy and then having three active toddlers, we haven't gotten around to setting up the playroom the way we want yet. Only just started playing again recently for the first time in two fucking years."

"I'll bet that was rough. But I've been thinking about installing one in Cassie's studio too. We'd be able to do more on our mountain than at the ranch."

Adam saw definite possibilities for speeding his plans along if the two of them could work with their wives more often. He glanced up at the hook again. "I was thinking I could arrange with Grant to have a demo at the Masters at Arms, if you think Cassie would be comfortable with that."

"Hmm. Now that's going to take a little more work. Not just with me perfecting my rigging skills, but with Cassie's comfort level for anything more than private play. But Ryder keeps trying to get us to join them at Gunnar Larson's home dungeon sometime."

"I'm sure Gunnar would make sure everything was safe too." He'd mentored both Grant and Damián in various BDSM skills, and along with Adam, had helped them become excellent dominants.

"Good to know. I don't know him, but Ryder swears Gunnar's a great mentor."

Adam wasn't aware that the man did rope, though. "He does rigging?"

"No, but there's a master rigger who shows up on occasion that I could possibly get some lessons with."

"Who?"

Luke gave him the name, one Adam was familiar with, thankfully. "He's good. I'm sure you can learn a lot from him, and since we're two hours apart, that'll help speed things along in getting Cassie ready for what I'd like to do at the club."

"I'll let you know when I think Cassie's ready to play rope bunny in front of a crowd." Luke shook his head and grinned. "If you'd asked me that three years ago, I'd say that would be about when hell froze over. But she trusts me and loves rope now. I think she's begun to trust you, too, more than she used to, anyway."

"Not sure what I ever did to make her so skittish around me, but she sure has come a long way."

Luke shot him a grin. "I guess love heals."

Lord knew Adam had healed all kinds of wounds he wasn't even aware he'd harbored, thanks to the love of Karla and his family. Not that he wanted to discuss that shit now.

"I'd say you've done a lot to make Cassie more comfortable around me."

Luke shrugged. "Just took some time for her to see we aren't all bad. I know she sees how much you love Karla, and that's probably why she doesn't see you as a threat anymore. Besides, it wasn't just you, but men in general—and for good reason."

Karla had never told him the details about Cassie's past, but knowing what her mission was here at the ranch, he could surmise. Adam understood how PTSD could cripple a person's life, but Cassie had overcome a lot of her issues in the past few years.

"Keep me posted on your progress, Luke. I'm sure Grant will welcome us doing a demo anytime. She's never been much into rope."

"Yeah, I guess rope would be rather tame for her."

"Got that right." Although Adam could definitely picture the Domme using rope as a torture device.

"Now, I'd like to keep what we talked about today a surprise from Karla and Cassie until we're ready to do this demo at the club."

"You do know keeping secrets between them will be impossible."

Adam sighed. "Yeah, you're right. Okay, maybe we need to make them think we're working on one thing while we're actually preparing them for something bigger."

Luke thought a moment. "I think just asking Karla to be there as moral support for a newbie rope bunny would raise no suspicions for Cassie."

"Excellent idea."

"I won't mention anything to Grant until we're sure it's a go, but you're damned good with rope already, Luke, especially shibari. Now we just need to get you up to speed on some of the safer, more functional, ties we use in suspension."

"Always excited to learn more from a master rigger like you."

Adam brushed off the compliment. "You'll be mentoring others in a few years, I guarantee it."

The triangular dinner bell rang, calling them back to the house.

"I can't remember the last time we ate inside the house," Luke remarked. "Usually we have so many ranch guests, we eat with them in the event barn. But Ryder and I have decided to leave Saturday afternoons and all day Sunday free for us to spend time with our wives. More than a thousand guests have passed through here since we opened."

"Wow! I had no idea! But you're right to remember to take time to recharge."

Luke nodded. "And it'll make us much more effective in our mission here at the ranch too."

"It's a great service you're offering to those with physical and emotional challenges in their lives, but you don't want to become casualties of your good deeds."

The Dreams Found Ranch had begun by rehabilitating neglected and abused mustangs, but they'd soon learned the horses could then help veterans and first responders dealing with PTSD, as well as children and adults trying to overcome injuries, illnesses, or birth defects that make it difficult to do activities most people took for granted.

"Most leave here better than they were when they came," Luke said, "and many come more than once a year."

"I've noticed a big change in Ryder too," Adam mentioned.

He'd been shocked when his brother-in-law and fellow Marine had attended Marc and Angelina's wedding. While Ryder hadn't made it to the reception, Megan had told him about several events out here on the ranch where Ryder had been able to handle the crowds without having any adverse effects. "He seems to be thriving."

Luke nodded. "You should have seen him and Megan line dancing at the farewell party Friday night."

"Damn!" Adam couldn't picture it, but the image he formed in his head pleased him. "Thanks for taking a chance on having Ryder and Megan join you in this venture."

"I wouldn't have been able to do a fraction of this without them."

"I'll admit, I was worried about their future when she first told me they'd gotten married. Ryder's as good as they come, but combat trauma can mess with a man's head."

And wasn't that the understatement of the century?

Adam's own issues had been under control the past couple of years, but he'd been triggered by seeing all the blood streaming from Pax's wound two weeks ago. He'd thought having Karla and the kids to anchor him—not to mention his new business—had put any remaining post-traumatic stress episodes behind him. Until then, Adam hadn't had one since Marc's interrogation scene a few years back. Unlike Damián, Marc, and Ryder, he'd opted out of therapy and treatment, choosing to manage any episodes on his own. He'd been doing fine—until Pax's injury.

Had Karla noticed this episode? Hopefully, she'd simply thought he was inept in handling an emergency involving one of his kids.

Or maybe she thought it a bit of both.

Bringing himself back to the present when Luke said, "It's an added bonus that Ryder can relate to the combat vets when they come here. And Cassie talks with survivors of rape and violent assaults. Of course, Megan's always great with the kids, sharing her love of photography and going on trail rides with them."

Luke opened the gate, and Adam preceded him into the yard. "So the community we've brought together at the ranch is a godsend for us as well as our guests."

"Daddy! Daddy! Daddy!" A chorus of high-pitched screams went up from his three munchkins, who came running from the front porch to greet him. He scooped all three up in his arms, kissing each in turn.

"Can I have a horsie, Daddy?" Kate asked.

"Wide the 'pacas, Daddy? Pweez?" Pax begged.

"Daddy, Hero's hungry too!" Rori informed him.

"Whoa, there! One at a time!" Adam would never tamp down their exuberance, but that didn't mean he'd give in to all their demands.

Karla came up to him and kissed him on the cheek. "You were out there a long time."

He grinned. "We're cooking up some plans for you and Cassie."

She nibbled the inside of her lower lip. She probably thought they were talking new kink furniture. "Are you sure Cas—"

"That's for Luke and me to worry about, Kitten."

She thought about his words a moment, then smiled. "I know you'll both be gentle with her." Karla would be an asset when it came to easing Cassie into the plan too.

Adam put the kids down and each grabbed one of their parents' hands as they walked inside ahead of Luke. "I fed the trips and put out some new coloring books and crayons to occupy them while we eat in relative peace."

Adam bent down to kiss her cheek, then whispered, "From your mouth to God's ears."

*   *   *

Cassie

Cassie didn't want to leave the bathroom with her red-rimmed eyes, but Luke had already knocked on the door once to see if she needed anything. She'd been in here for close to twenty minutes.

Removing the cold, wet washcloth from her eyes, she inspected the damage. Still red and puffy. But she and Luke would be heading to bed soon. Maybe he wouldn't notice. She left the bathroom with her eyes downcast and crossed the room to go straight to their bed. In a signal that she wasn't interested in making love tonight, she didn't remove her gown.

But Luke was nowhere to be seen. He must have gone back downstairs.

Good.

She quickly slipped between the sheets and curled onto her side, away from where Luke would lie. Perhaps she could feign sleep before—

"Everything okay, Sweet Pea?" His presence dominated the room, and a shiver went down her spine at his nearness. A quick peek as he walked across the room showed her he wore nothing but his undershorts.

"Yes. Just drained after so much excitement today. Being an introvert is exhausting sometimes."

"It was great seeing Adam, Karla, and the kids, though. You and Megan did an awful lot of work preparing everything. Thank you, Sweet Pea." He crawled into the bed behind her and spooned up against her backside, giving her a kiss on her neck. "We'll take it easy tomorrow."

Feeling his warm body against her almost made her want to ask him to make love tonight, but in her current mood, she didn't think it would be very satisfying for him. Better not to try at all rather than disappoint him any further.

His arm stroked hers. "You sure everything's all right? You've been awfully quiet since we got home."

Her throat closed up, making spoken words impossible, so she merely nodded. But Luke tugged at her upper arm until she lay on her back staring up at him.

A line formed between his brows. "You've been crying." She could never keep anything from him. "What's wrong, baby girl?" He brushed the hair away from her face, but his endearment left a bigger ache in her chest. Seeing the pain in his eyes hurt even more. "Did something happen today that I missed while I was out in the shop with Adam?"

She shook her head vehemently. "No, nothing happened. It was all so wonder—" She choked on the word, and the tears began flowing again. She closed her eyes, knowing her crying would hurt him and yet unable to stop.

"Shh." He kissed her forehead and pulled her against his warm body, sheltering her. "Just let it out. I've got you, Sweet Pea."

Luke never failed to be there when she needed him. He had done so much for her when she'd struggled to overcome her past. Why couldn't she give him back the thing he wanted more than anything?

After her sobs subsided several minutes later, Luke brushed the tears from her cheeks. "Now, tell me what has you so upset." His voice had become deeper and more authoritative. When he used that voice, she had a hard time refusing his commands.

Drawing a deep breath, she allowed the words to spill out. "I fear I may never be able to give you a son or daughter."

Luke separated himself from her and leaned on his elbow while searching her face. "That's what has you upset? Sweet Pea, haven't we talked about this before? The doctor hasn't found any reason for us not to be pregnant, so I don't want you blaming yourself for one minute."

"But your sperm counts are fine. The doctor called them Supermen. My eggs must be the problem. Perhaps we should try in vitro one more time."

He drew a slow, deep breath, shaking his head. "Cassie, it killed me to see the pain they put you through that first time. I can't do that again."

The experience had been horrific only to be told that no babies would result from the technique.

Luke stroked her cheek with his thumb, and she felt the coldness of her tears. "Whether we're blessed with children or not didn't matter to me, until tonight when I realized this is still weighing heavily on your mind."

"Perhaps seeing Karla with their children—and watching you play with them after dinner—just did something to me today. I'd hate it if we could never have children of our own for you to play with and raise."

"Nothin' wrong with being Uncle Luke to other people's kids. I can spoil them then send them home to their parents." Luke's boyish grin brought a half smile to her face too.

Cassie placed her hand at the nape of his neck and brought his face closer to kiss him.

"I love you so much, Luke."

"You know I'd do anything in this world to keep hearing you saying that, Sweet Pea. I'm one helluva lucky man. My life is complete with you in it. And we have the horses, alpacas, and dogs who are like our babies."

Her husband would never out and out lie to her, so maybe she had been fretting over something that truly didn't matter to him.

Luke stretched out beside her again, and she nestled her head in the crook of his shoulder, while her hand idly played with the fine hairs in the center of his chest. For whatever reason, though, she still wasn't ready to abandon this conversation. "Do you ever imagine us with children, though?"

"Let's not beat a dead horse, baby. I'm perfectly content to have you and our animals, not to mention our honorary nieces and nephew."

Perhaps she'd phrased the question wrong. "I mean, I guess I'm wondering if you've ever thought about adopting a baby." She'd never brought it up before now, but then neither had he.

Luke remained silent for a long moment, and she feared she should have kept her thoughts to herself.

Finally, Luke took her by the chin and turned her face upward to meet his gaze. "Last night, I had a dream—maybe a vision even. You were holding the hand of a little girl with a colorful shawl over her head covered by a red hat. Her long, jet-black hair reminded me of yours."

He described a photo he'd seen of her as a child in traditional Peruvian regalia, similar to what she'd worn on her church wedding day. Luke sometimes had visions of the future—like the one that had involved her before she'd ever met him.

Again, her throat closed as her eyes welled with tears. Luke so wanted a child of their own. What if she couldn't give him that?

Luke idly stroked her cheek, waiting for a response. He always gave her extra time to formulate her words. Then something occurred to her.

Wait a minute.

"The girl in your vision looked like *me*?" Not a mix of her and Luke, but Cassie's Spanish and Quechua mixed heritage alone?

"Spitting image. And I've been with you long enough to know to take signs and visions seriously, baby girl." The two of them were connected to the universe in a significant way for certain. They wouldn't be together today if not for some serious cosmic interventions. "I just didn't give it much thought. Figured when the time was right, we'd discuss becoming parents. Then you brought up having kids tonight."

Perhaps they couldn't have biological babies of their own, but adoption might be an option. "In Peru, Luke, many children are abandoned by their mothers, whether for financial, cultural, or other reasons." She sighed. "Most are of mixed race—often Quechua and Spanish, like me."

"That breaks my heart." The anguish in his eyes spoke volumes.

He'd grown to love her country during their twice-a-year visits there. "I'm glad your parents were able to keep you and Eduardo."

She nodded. "As am I. They loved each other so much that they never gave the haters any power over their lives."

"You mean you faced that prejudice too?"

She shrugged it off, although she did feel as if she was somewhere between the two worlds growing up.

"Talk to me, Sweet Pea. Did you have it rough growing up in your village?"

She shook her head. "Not as badly as some. My parents were well respected there, which helped."

Cassie wouldn't recount the times she'd been the butt of a racial slur, though, because there was no point. Water under the bridge, as they said in America. But was the situation for today's little children the same, better, or worse? Somehow with all the racial hatred in the world, she expected it to be worse. And she wasn't sure how accepting the people here in Colorado would be to a brown-skinned girl. Sometimes Cassie had been told to go home by some bigots who judged her by the color of her skin, but she wouldn't acknowledge them in any way.

"If you want to adopt," Luke began, "I'm open to bringing one of those forgotten children into our home. Every child deserves a loving home."

His words warmed her heart and pushed any negative thoughts away.

"How old was the little girl in your vision?"

"About J.D.'s age, I guess. I don't know if I was seeing this in the near future or years away, though."

"If we did adopt one of these lost children, does it matter to you whether it is an older child rather than a baby?"

"Not at all. One of the benefits of adopting an older child would be that they'd have ready-made cousins close in age."

She smiled as a vision flitted through her mind of their own little girl—or boy—playing with Karla's and Savannah's children, chasing after the alpacas and dogs here on their mountain. Riding horses at the ranch. Petting the new crias. "Oh, Luke, now you have me picturing your vision."

"All of 'em playing with the alpacas in the shed?"

She leaned on her elbow, eyes opened wide. "How did you know? I pictured them with the new crias, including a little girl who looks like me."

He grinned, melting her heart. "Darlin', don't you know we are connected on every level imaginable? I think somebody up there," he pointed toward the ceiling and the heavens—"is trying to get our attention. Why don't we look into an adoption on our next trip to Peru?"

They'd just been to Peru in February but wouldn't be returning until December. "At Christmas?"

"I didn't think about how far away that is. Maybe we can start the process online, and if we need to make a special trip sooner than that, we will. We can ask Dakota or Matt to help out at the ranch while we're gone."

"They were a big help to Ryder and Megan the last time we went to visit your family.

Thoughts of starting the adoption process were both daunting and exciting at the same time. She didn't have the first idea where to start.

Cassie pulled her husband closer and kissed him. "Have I told you lately how much I adore you, Lucas Denton?"

"Sweet Pea, you show me that every damned day."

Her need to feel a closer bond with him tonight made her ask, "Would you tie me up tonight?"

* * *

Luke

Hot damn!

He hadn't expected this tonight. "You know it, darlin'."

But his lovely wife wanted to be tied up. She didn't have to ask him twice. That she'd come to think of rope as a way to relieve stress and build a closer bond with him suited him just fine.

Maybe he could practice some of the ties he and Adam had talked about earlier. He'd practiced them before on a chest mannequin in Cassie's studio, just not on his lovely wife.

"Strip for me, Sweet Pea."

While he loved the beauty and artistry of shibari and other forms of decorative rope work, tonight he intended to tie her up and tease her body into a frenzy.

Luke's gaze remained transfixed on her as she knelt in the center of the bed and lifted the silky gown over her head. *Naked.* She usually wore nothing to bed, so he was glad to be rid of even that flimsy barrier between their bodies.

Luke took her hand and helped her off the bed to stand next to it. A beam of moonlight came through the skylight and zeroed in on her breasts, high and firm, as they awaited his pleasure.

First things first.

He cupped her breasts, pinching her nipples to two taut peaks. Her hiss of breath excited him. Clearly, she was ready.

Still, he couldn't resist bending down to plant a kiss on each nipple. His tongue licked one, making lazy circles around the areola before he covered it with his mouth and sucked—hard. She gasped.

He'd surprised her. *Oh how I love doing that.* He had more surprises in store for her too.

"You know your slow-down and safewords, Sweet Pea. Don't hesitate to use them if you need to."

The hitch in her breathing betrayed her excitement, as well as some nerves, which made his dominant heart happy. Once she'd finally come to trust him, he'd treasured her beautiful submission each and every time. Cassie had used her safeword in the past, so he had every expectation that she would again tonight, if needed.

Not that he thought this would be too much for her, given what they'd done in the past. But he could never predict when a buried trigger might catch them off guard. They'd worked on so many of them, with the advice of Savannah and Cassie's therapist, though, that Luke hoped there wouldn't be any others.

Luke left her standing while he went to the corner of the room to pull out four bundles of rope from the basket he kept there. Tucking three bundles under his arm, he made eye contact with her as he crossed the room, loosening the first one. She continued to worry her lower lip. Her heightened nerves would make this more enjoyable for them both.

He draped the loosened rope around her neck and let it fall over her breasts to tease her nipples. Stalking her like prey, he walked circles around her before taking the next bundle and loosening it to add to the first. Eventually, all four bundles were draped around her neck. He wanted to introduce her to the rope she'd soon be bound with, intimately and thoroughly.

"Hands in the box-tie position at your lower back." Moving into position, she pushed her breasts out for him. Slipping one of the lengths of rope from around her neck, he separated the remaining strands to expose her nipples again. Luke wound one end of the rope around his left hand and the other around his right. Making fists, he yanked the rope taut, then rubbed the soft strands up and down over her breasts several times to stimulate her nipples.

Cassie looked down at the rope and the effect it had on her.

"Look at me, darlin'." She complied immediately. "I want you to become one with the rope, imagining it hugging at every part of your body in intimate ways. To see the rope as another lover here to bring you pleasure."

They locked eyes as Luke slid the rope down her abdomen to

her mound, but he didn't linger there. Not yet. Instead, he continued over her thighs, knees, and calves. Finally, he let that rope drop onto the tops of her feet. Picking up one end, he moved behind her and tied a knot a few inches from her wrists, careful to avoid the delicate bones there.

Luke let the loose end of the rope dangle to the floor as he took a second rope. He wrapped it around his fists again, but this time, he slid the taut rope down her back from her shoulder blades, over the small of her back, and then paid special attention to the curve of her ass. Gooseflesh broke out on her body where the rope had kissed her skin.

Moving to stand in front of her again, he smiled when Cassie's breathing became rapid and shallow. Her pupils dilated, and her nipples remained hard despite the lack of further stimulation in the past few minutes.

My girl is ready for me.

Section Four

Cassie

Cassie's body buzzed with electricity and excitement. Luke had a feral look in his eyes tonight, as if he stalked her as prey. His primal focus on her sent shivers down her spine.

I need this!

He worked silently, wrapping her chest in rope above and below her breasts. She couldn't see what he was doing behind her. Cassie expected him to do something more elaborate, but after he secured a rope over her shoulders, he crisscrossed it with an X between her breasts and then returned to stand in front of her.

Her bare nipples ached, silently begging for his fingers and lips to touch her again, but he didn't. Cassie became so wet, she couldn't wait to take him inside her body to return some of the love he was showing her.

But Luke didn't seem to be in any hurry. She stood before him with grace, exactly the way he'd taught her to present herself to him years ago. Her trust deepened every time they played.

Luke gathered up the ends of the two remaining ropes and tugged on them until she followed him to the bed. The two of them never broke eye contact.

"I'll help you get on your side in the middle of the bed."

With Luke's strong hands supporting her, Cassie eased into position. They'd discovered early on that having her hands tied behind her back and then having to lie on her back was extremely uncomfortable. As always, Luke learned her likes and dislikes and remembered them.

He wasted no time in taking her left ankle and pulling it up against the back of her thigh. Would he do something intricate or make quick work with the leg ties so that they could move on to other things? Her heart skipped a beat at the thought of what was to come.

He wrapped her calf and thigh together. "Is that too tight, Sweet Pea?"

"No. The rope actually feels amazing."

He chuckled and went back to slipping the rope in and out of the design. As his fingers brushed her bare upper thigh, oh so close to her private area—her *pussy*, as Luke wanted her to call it—Cassie felt a jolt of electricity run straight to her clit. He'd worked hard these past three years to replace any horrid memories of the rape with much more loving touches connected only to him.

Luke helped me reclaim my body and my sexuality.

Once he'd completed that tie, he moved on to her other leg and did much the same. This three-band tie was a new one for him. She liked the diamond-shape he'd left in the center of the bands. Luke always added such beautiful flourishes to his ties.

"Now, let me get you into position." Luke lifted her upper body until she was in an upright, seated position near the headboard with her knees resting on two pillows. He then took another rope, or perhaps the end of the one he'd used to tie her chest harness, and looped it through one of the bands, then tugged her left leg up, spreading her open. Soon, her right leg was equally positioned, leaving her pussy exposed and ready for whatever Luke had in mind.

Can he see how wet I am for him?

Cassie's entire body thrummed with anticipation. Luke stood and walked to the foot of the bed, turning to stare at her. First her face, smiling at her before his gaze slowly lowered to her bare breasts. In the rope bra of sorts, her bare nipples peaked. Then his gaze moved even lower.

Cassie had no worries about being in such a vulnerable position, because every time Luke had tied her up and she'd surrendered her defenses, he had put her needs first and foremost. Sometimes he seemed to know her boundaries better than she did.

I trust him.

Luke glanced at the bedposts, cocked his head to one side, and walked toward the head of the bed. She couldn't see what he was doing, but felt a tug at the rope in the center of her back. Was he planning to tie her chest harness to the bed?

Without any clues or explanations, he went back to the basket in the corner of the room to take out two more bundles, loosening the rope of one then the other as he sauntered toward her. The sense of being stalked came to mind again, but the sultry look in his eyes only ignited her passion even more.

When he reached her side, he connected both ropes to the back of her chest harness and spread out the ends on either side of her. "Lean back against the headboard, baby girl."

She did as instructed, and he pulled the first loose end tight to secure her upper body to one bedpost before walking around the bed to the other side to do the same with the other.

"Now, relax into the rope, Sweet Pea."

After doing so, she realized she'd been tensing her body to remain upright. Now, with the rope holding her firmly in place, she could relax.

"That's it, Sweet Pea." Luke stroked her face before stripping out of his clothes and joining her on the bed.

She couldn't help but wonder what position he had in mind for having sex with her in her current state of bondage. Her weight rested on her knees, her heels against her butt, lifting her pussy off the mattress five or six inches. But her legs were spread wide open for whatever he had in mind.

Luke rolled onto his back, giving her a good view of his erect cock, which made her pussy clench and weep in anticipation. He stared up at her and smiled. Did he notice?

Please, Luke, don't make me wait for it!

Totally surprising her, he tilted his head back while reaching up to tweak her nipples. She wished he would take them in his mouth again, but that wouldn't be possible in his current position.

Cassie closed her eyes, letting the intense need for him wash over her. She wanted to stroke his hair and run her hands down his body before grasping his cock and going down on him, but she wasn't free to move.

Using his feet to shove himself up the mattress and closer to her, he wedged his mouth directly under her pussy and nibbled at her lower lips before his tongue pushed inside her.

"Oh, yes, Luke!"

He chuckled with his face pressed against her so that she felt the vibration to her very core, then his tongue retreated only to push inside her again. The beard he'd started to grow in the last two weeks scratched against her sensitive skin, adding an element she hadn't expected. But his playfulness made her worry, because he didn't seem to be in any hurry to take her over the edge tonight.

Still able to tilt her pelvis ever so slightly, she ground herself against his nose, mouth, and chin, trying to encourage him to focus on her clit.

Instead, Luke stopped moving and slid out from under her. "Baby girl, who is in control of this pussy?"

She groaned inside. "You are."

"Then I expect you to remain perfectly still and let me do my job."

"Yes, Sir."

Luke rarely required her to use dominant/submissive protocols, but his tone brooked no argument this time. She wanted to please him as he pleasured her.

"Good girl." He resumed his delightful plundering of her nether regions. She bit her bottom lip to keep from screaming in frustration, though.

After an interminable time, finally he wrapped his lips around her waiting bundle of nerves.

Yes!

Squeezing her eyes tightly closed, she forced air into her lungs after realizing she'd stopped breathing for a few seconds.

Luke sucked and pulled on her clit.

"Oh Goddess! That feels so good!"

Surely her juices dripped all over his lower face, but he didn't stop. When his hand came toward her pussy, she held her breath again, wondering if he'd be able to slip his finger inside her wet pussy or touch her clit and stroke her to an orgasm. She'd rather have his cock, but how much time would it take to get her out of these ropes?

When not one but two fingers entered her, she bucked onto his hand involuntarily, then quickly regained her position so that he wouldn't stop.

Another chuckle reverberated through her. Luke was enjoying torturing her.

A third finger entered her, and he began pumping them in and out as his tongue lashed her clit mercilessly. She needed to come, but wouldn't demand anything he wasn't ready to give her. Luke always made sure her needs were met; he just didn't always do it in the time she wanted.

Please, Lucas! I cannot wait much longer!

Luke lowered his head, breaking contact. "Get ready, baby girl."

His whiskers and lips nuzzled her inner thigh before his tongue laved the length of her vulva. *Pussy!* So close! The tip of his tongue flicked against her clit, lashing it like a flogger, and he plunged what felt like three fingers inside her.

The rush of sensations all at once sent her flying over the edge.

"Yes! I'm coming! Please don't stop!"

Cassie rode the crest as long as she could, but all too soon the stroke of his tongue became almost painful. "No more! I cannot take any more, Sir."

Luke moved away from her clit. "Oh, I think my girl can take it a little bit more for me."

How much longer could she stand it with her clit so hypersensitive? Usually, he stopped right after he'd made her come so that she could recoup and they could make love. She wanted him to reach orgasm too.

"I'll try," she squeaked out. Again, he applied mouth, tongue, and fingers to tease and torment her to the point of screaming in near pain. Kitty told her once about how Adam tortured her with orgasms. Is that what the two men were plotting for so long out at the corral and in Luke's studio? Did they talk to each other about what they did to their wives and compare notes?

Just when she thought she could take no more, though, another wave crested and she exploded again.

"Oh, Goddess! Yes!!!"

When he pulled away this time, he turned over and got onto his knees facing her.

"Is the Goddess really responsible for those two orgasms, Sweet Pea?"

Cassie blushed. "Oh no, Sir. That was all your doing. Thank you so much, but now it's time for me to pleasure you."

His expression grew stern, and she remembered herself. "I mean, if you'd like me to, Sir."

She lapsed easily into her submissive role whenever he went all Dom on her.

Oh, how I love my man.

*   *   *

Luke

Later that night, Cassie slept peacefully, curled up against his body as they spooned with Luke's arm draped over her waist, his hand cupping her breast. He couldn't imagine life without his girl.

Tonight, he'd tried some new ties with her before they'd made love. Jeezus, he'd come so hard, he didn't think he'd ever stop. Her screams spurred him on as she came yet again. Clearly, she'd enjoyed their time together as much as he had. He always tried to make it better for her than for him, but she turned the tables on him with her hands, mouth, and pussy, and he couldn't wait to do it again.

Thoughts of what they'd talked about earlier came back into his mind. While he hadn't given up on having biological babies of their own, the thought of giving one of those Peruvian cast-off kids a home here on their mountain warmed his heart. Having a little girl the spitting image of Cassie running around turned his heart into a big ol' pile of mush. That glimpse of heaven had been so vivid, he almost felt as if he'd been seeing mother and daughter.

After three years of trying to get pregnant, it was time to take an alternate journey to parenthood. They had enough love to open their hearts and their home to someone in need of their love and shelter.

Cassie would make a wonderful mother, and he'd do everything in his power to adore and protect any child they were blessed with, biological or adopted.

He wondered how long the adoption process would take. At least Cassie had dual citizenship, which might give them a leg up on other Americans seeking to adopt from Peru. How perfect would that be for them?

And given how the little girl in his vision had looked just like his wife, Luke hoped they'd be paired with a little girl, but he'd welcome a little boy too. Maybe even one of each.

Whoa, there, boy! Let's take this one kid at a time.

Still, he couldn't wait to tell Ryder and Megan about their plans. Maybe he would spark the idea with them to do something similar. Ryder didn't talk about it, but seeing them interact with the triplets as well as Marisol and J.D. when they visited, no doubt they would enjoy having kids of their own too.

Luke smiled as he closed his eyes. Could life get any better for his newfound family?

*   *   *

Ryder

"Have you ever thought about adopting?" Megan asked after they'd finished making love this morning.

Ryder turned toward her as she pulled her shirt on, covering her sexy body from his view. God, the woman turned him on. He could go again if they didn't have new arrivals coming in a couple of hours.

Ryder forced his mind back to her question.

"Adopting what, Red?" He didn't think the ranch could sustain many more rescued mustangs, although Matt Giardano had agreed to help them out with some now that he and Dakota were engaged, and she'd be sticking around his place.

She stared at him, scrunching up her brows as if he'd grown a second head. "A *baby*, silly. Or even an older child, maybe."

They hadn't talked about adopting kids in a long time, because they'd been so busy running the Dreams Found Ranch. Where would they find the time and energy for babies or kids?

Apparently, Megan had been thinking about it, though.

"You're so good with kids," Megan continued, "and I can't give you any babies myself, so I just wondered if—"

He held up a hand. Thoughts of having the responsibility for a little person who depended on him completely scared him a little.

"I'm good with loving on other people's kids for now. Not sure I'm cut out to have any of my own yet." At her stricken look, he moved closer to her. "Not saying I've ruled them out forever. We've just had so much else going on that I haven't given it any thought. Between ranch guests and rescued horses, do you think we can take on that kind of responsibility now?"

Megan smiled, and her body relaxed. "You're absolutely right. And that's a relief to hear, really. It's just that, when I see you with Adam's or Damián's kids, I worry that I'm depriving you of experiencing an important aspect of life."

Was she serious? He wrapped her in his arms. "Red, you're all the family I'll ever need. If we're both ready to adopt someday, we'll do it, but right now, I'm enjoying the extended honeymoon with you." He kissed her long and slow, tasting her lips until he almost told her to strip down again so they could go back to bed.

"I'm not ready to take that step either, Ryder, but wanted to make sure you weren't feeling left out."

"Never. I love kids, but they are a life-altering proposition, and it's best to think it through before committing to something we can't give back if we aren't ready." He thought a moment and added, "Anytime you want to offer our babysitting services to get a little practice in, though, I'm all for it. Now that the triplets are older, they can probably spend the night with us every now and then. I'm sure Adam and Karla would love to have some time alone again." He imagined they'd love to have a trip to the kink club Adam used to run, although from what he'd heard, Adam had his own setup at home using some of Luke's dual-purpose furniture.

"When we go to the Deadwood cabin, why don't we take our bigger tent and let the triplets camp out with us?" She laughed at her own question. "That would sure be a test of our parenting abilities." The extended Gallagher and Montague family would be spending a week together there in August.

"Sounds like fun to me." While Ryder's anxiety issues had subsided—in large part due to the equine therapy he received here and talking regularly with his counselor in the Veterans Administration—he suspected Megan still worried about his becoming overwhelmed around too many people in close quarters. No doubt she'd suggested camping out for that reason. How big could the cabin be?

"I'm also hoping for us to escape to a private area to pitch our tent on your family's ancestral lands so I can have my way with you, Red."

Megan's smile grew wider. "That can be arranged too. I'll purchase train tickets for the rest of them to ride the narrow-gauge railroad," she said as she kissed him. "Then we'll have our tent and the property to ourselves for a few hours."

"I like how you think, woman."

"We can camp alone up there every night, if you'd like."

"Consider it a date."

This would be the first time Ryder had gone to the cabin. Megan had shared so many childhood memories of the time spent there with Patrick and their parents. Patrick had bought the property from their mother, with Megan's blessing because neither she nor her mother had any desire to live there. Apparently, they hadn't even been up there since the deed changed hands.

That Megan was content living here with him outside Fairchance pleased him.

But having three little kids for one night in a tent certainly wouldn't make him panic. They handled kids here at the ranch all the time. In fact, they expected a busload from Big Brothers and Big Sisters in Denver this morning.

Speaking of which, city kids were always eager to learn about the ranch and hit the ground running. Ryder could put them to work mucking the stalls, which should buy him and Megan a little more time alone this morning.

Megan kissed his lower lip, apparently not quite ready to face the day, either. When he opened his mouth to welcome her, she slid her tongue inside. Grabbing the back of her head, he held her in place as he deepened the kiss.

Clearly, they weren't going to make it to the barn before this week's arrivals showed up, because right now, he had one sexy wife he needed to satisfy and love on.

Section Five

Karla

"**I**'m higha than clouds, Mommy! Like Supaman!" Pax pressed his nose against the window while seated on Karla's lap as they flew on Patrick's private jet to Chicago to pick up Adam's mom and former mother-in-law. Karla might never want to fly commercial again.

"Isn't this neat, sweetie?" Karla stroked his soft cheek, noticing that his run-in with the scissors had barely left a mark on his temple. "I'll bet you didn't think you'd ever be flying above the clouds, did you?"

A sudden sadness came over Karla as she thought about her brother, Ian, for whom Pax had been named. The clouds made her think of heaven where she knew he must be raising some hell at this very moment. God, she'd missed him these past four years.

Don't go there. Ian stays with you in spirit.

Megan entertained Rori with a book while Ryder and Kate played Candyland at the conference table closer to the cockpit door. Adam had been in the cockpit with Patrick since takeoff in Denver, probably talking about their recent escapade where his brother had helped him out on an assignment requiring air transportation.

She'd expected Adam's security business to keep him closer to home, but this case involved a Marine buddy in need of help. Adam couldn't turn him down and rightly so. Grant and Damián had also joined him on the mission. From what Adam had told her later, the situation had been taken care of and they'd gotten *satisfaction,* to use his words.

Whatever that means. Best not to ask.

He'd recently hired more people to join his firm, most of them veterans. After this recent mission, he'd even been trying to talk Master Gunnery Sergeant Richardson—who had attended their wedding with his wife—into moving from California to help. So far, he hadn't convinced the Marine to come out of retirement or make the move. But Adam had been rejuvenated by being with his Marine Corps brothers again. Perhaps they should plan a trip to visit his old friends in Southern California sometime now that the kids were old enough to travel more.

Adam never went into great detail about any of his clients with her, although she had learned he'd managed to provide the fire investigation unit with surveillance footage that everyone hoped would lead to an arrest in the arson cases plaguing the city now. While the nightclub Adam provided surveillance for hadn't burned, a nearby business down the block had. The surveillance cameras had spooked the guy. Apparently, to show his gratitude, the bar owner had paid him a large bonus that he was able to share with those who had helped on the case. She couldn't complain.

Not out loud, anyway. The money had helped them too.

Pax laid his head against her chest, continuing to watch the clouds go by, his eyelids drooping. Karla's began to grow heavy as well. Getting everyone ready for this trip had exhausted her. Adam helped when he was home, but he'd had a lot of catching up to do after that long-distance mission and had picked up new clients. Business was good. Thank goodness he hadn't bowed out from this trip. They needed time away from day-to-day responsibilities, although they'd brought their most important ones with them, of course.

Pax's weight was lifted off her, and Karla opened her eyes to see Adam smiling down as he cradled a sleeping Pax. "Sorry I had to wake you, Kitten, but it's time to get everyone ready for the descent into Chicago."

He strapped the still sleeping boy into his car seat in front of them facing toward Karla. Ryder and Megan were seeing that Rori and Kate were secured into their car seats across the aisle.

"I must have conked out for a while."

Adam took his spot beside her in the leather-covered seat and kissed her cheek. "You have to be exhausted after the last few days."

"It'll all be worth it when we get there. Good thing I never have trouble sleeping. I just have to close my eyes."

He took her hand and brought it to his lips. "I'll see that you get lots of rest this week."

Karla smiled, wondering how he thought he'd manage that feat with so many people crammed into the tiny cabin where they'd spent their honeymoon. Ryder and Megan had brought camping gear and offered to let the kids pile in with them at least one night to see how they'd do away from their parents. But with five other adults in a one-bedroom cabin, including Adam's mother and former mother-in-law, Karla didn't expect anyone to get a lot of sleep.

She'd have thought over the past three years she'd have found ways to catch up on sleep by now, but the kids were growing more independent and wouldn't be this young forever. She hated to miss a moment by taking time to sleep.

Karla had learned the hard way that life was too short.

*   *   *

Adam

"You've done a helluva job with the place, Patrick." Adam couldn't believe his eyes. The renovations had been far more extensive than Patrick had let on or than Adam had pictured.

While Patrick had kept the integrity of the original cabin's central room mostly intact, he'd converted a window along the back wall into a door that led to a hallway and two additional bedrooms, from what Adam had seen on the outside.

His brother started working on the place again about three years ago and now lived half the year here; the other half he spent along the Central Coast of California. Adam hadn't a clue how much he'd accomplished since his and Karla's honeymoon. He'd been impressed with all Patrick had done even then, but the rustic, falling-down cabin of his childhood was becoming quite the showplace.

"You've tripled the size of the cabin," their mother remarked.

Patrick chuckled. "I had some downtime the past few years before starting up my flight business last spring, Mom, so I spent much of it up here. I find this a good place to unwind and regroup. Besides, I love working with my hands."

"I don't see how you had any time for unwinding, but good job." Adam clapped him on the shoulder blade before glancing out the window to where the toddlers were running circles around Ryder. When they weren't climbing onto his back, they appeared to be somewhat helpful by handing him tent spikes.

"Our family is expanding, thanks to you and Karla," Patrick said, "and I wanted to make sure we can accommodate everyone. Maybe this will become an annual get-together."

"That would be great. I have a lot of good memories here." He stroked Karla's lower back, remembering their time here, but he'd also loved coming here as a kid, even though his mom had hated the place.

"I love this split level island, son," Mom called out from the modern kitchen that had replaced what used to be the bare minimum of equipment. She'd parked her wheelchair at one end of the granite surface. "Now I can help with food prep too." Of course, Patrick had made other parts of the cabin accessible for

Mom, too, from what Adam had seen. She'd learned to get around pretty well after nearly four decades, but these old structures weren't usually very accessible.

"Okay, our bags are in our room, Patricia" Marge said, coming down the hall from the new wing. Joni's mom had become part of the extended family and had been included in their get-togethers after she'd moved in with Mom in Chicago a couple of years ago.

"Let me stow our bags away, Kitten. Where do you want us, Patrick?"

"I figured you and Karla would want to take the original bedroom, where you spent your honeymoon." Patrick waggled his eyebrows.

Karla laughed. "I'm not sure we can get all the kids in there."

"But they're sleeping with us in the tent—at least tonight," Megan reminded her.

"They might start out in the tent," Karla countered, "but we need to have a backup plan just in case any or all of them change their minds in the middle of the night."

Adam thought having them help with putting up the tent might make them more committed to sleeping out there. But time would tell.

"Then why don't you take the new bedroom on the left?" Patrick asked. "Mom and Marge took the one across the hall with the twin beds."

That had better mean they'd have a bed big enough for him and Karla, not that they hadn't made a twin bed work for them before.

Adam lifted their two suitcases and carried them down the hall toward the back of the house. Inside the new bedroom, Adam found a queen-sized bed, a wardrobe, and a little sitting area with a rocking chair. He opened another door and found it led to an ensuite bathroom. French doors led to a patio where he could see a hot tub.

Patrick must use this as his master bedroom when he stayed

here. Nice bachelor pad. Adam wondered if he ever brought a woman here. With Patrick's good looks and single status, Adam had no doubt he did, although Patrick never talked about anyone special.

It's none of your business.

Now to get the rest of the kids' paraphernalia in here. No wonder they didn't take many trips anymore. They had to bring half the house with them, or Karla insisted that they did.

Adam returned to the living room just as Rori and Kate came running into the house chased by Pax. The girls giggled at their ability to outrun their brother. Megan and Ryder brought up the rear.

"Just you wait, Pax," Patrick told him. "My sister used to do that to me when we were little." He gave Megan a pointed look. "And look at me now." He focused on Pax again and pulled himself up to his full height, flexing his biceps."

"Wow, Unca Patwick! I want to get big and stwong like you!"

"Ahem, brother dear. I can still outrun you any day," Megan challenged.

"Dream on."

Adam had never experienced sibling rivalry until he had his own kids. Did the way Megan and Patrick taunt each other as adults mean the triplets would never outgrow this phase?

Adam noticed Kate had stopped running and looked around the room as if taking it all in. She always was so observant, especially in new places like this. Her gaze landed on the portrait of Johnny and Kate Montague hanging over the fireplace.

"My horse!"

The kid sure did want a horse of her own. It was all she ever talked about anymore.

"Not *your* horse, hon," Adam corrected her. "She belongs to the woman in the picture. You're named after her, by the way. She's your great-great-great grandmother."

Kate stomped her foot and scrunched her eyebrows together. "My boy horse! Whiskey!" All eyes in the room turned to the toddler in the midst of a meltdown.

"Someone sounds sleepy." Karla scooped up the cranky three-year-old and looked apologetically at her mother-in-law.

As if Mom hadn't dealt with a fussy kid before—namely him. Possibly Patrick and Megan too.

"But we'll call the horse Whiskey, if you'd like." Karla wasn't one to argue with a toddler over something so inconsequential.

"Whiskey!" Kate insisted. "It's his name. Whiskey, Whiskey, Whiskey!" If the kid had been on the floor, she'd have stomped her foot again for emphasis.

"If you will excuse us," Karla said to no one in particular, "I'll put Kate down for a nap. Be right back."

Adam watched Karla carry Kate down the hall, his gaze lingering on her ass. He hoped they'd manage to have a little bit of alone time this week, although he wouldn't hold his breath that the kids would manage to spend the entire night in the tent.

When she was out of sight, his gaze returned to the painting above the mantel. Adam didn't know what to think, but he could resolve one issue. "I think the name of the horse is written on the back of the portrait." The horse hadn't been part of the family lore passed down, so he didn't remember, even though he'd looked at the names on the back when he and Karla were here after their wedding.

Before he could start toward the mantel, Patrick chimed in. "Don't bother looking. Kate's right. The horse's name is Whiskey. I noticed it when I hung the portrait there."

Adam's glance shifted from his ancestor Kate to his daughter of the same name. That explained it. Patrick must have told her about Whiskey before.

* * *

Karla

"Kate's so funny." Karla laid awake in bed with Adam that night, blissfully alone for the first time all day, her head resting in the crook of his arm. "After her nap, she tried to rearrange things in the living room to *put them back the right way*, as she said."

Adam didn't say anything. Had he fallen asleep? Then he broke his silence. "She knew the name of the horse in the portrait."

"I'd like to know who talked about the horse around her. You know all three of them are like sieves at this point. They don't miss a thing."

"Maybe. Patrick's done a lot of renovating here, although he didn't seem sure of it until he looked on the back of the painting." Adam shook his head. "I just hope Joni isn't back to play more tricks on us."

Karla sat up so that she could meet his gaze to see if he was joking, but his eyes were dead serious. Maybe *dead* wasn't the right word to use in this circumstance. "Your first wife very clearly moved on the last time we stayed in this cabin. She promised. Well, that's how we interpreted the signs anyway. I don't think her spirit lingered. Why would she? Her objective was to get us together, and she certainly succeeded." She stopped rambling and took a breath. But once Joni had succeeded in helping to get the two of them together, Karla hadn't felt or heard Joni again.

Not wanting to think or talk about her predecessor tonight, Karla bent to place a kiss on his lips, but didn't want to initiate anything that might lead to a painfully silent orgasm for her. With so many people in the house, they would have to control themselves.

Doesn't mean I can't touch, though.

Karla settled herself against his shoulder again, her hand stroking his chest, drawing lazy circles around his nips.

"I'm probably letting my imagination run away with me," he

admitted. "Maybe the place is haunted, and the original Kate whispered that in her ear or something."

Karla's hand stilled; she could feel his heart beating harder against her fingertips. This was really bothering him. "Okay, now you're freaking me out a little." *More than a little.* "I'm not sure I want to share this place with a ghost or a spirit or anything otherworldly."

He chuckled. "Neither do I, Kitten." He kissed the top of her head. "You're probably right. Kate overheard something Patrick said when we arrived. She doesn't miss a thing."

"One day, she'll be a great asset to your security business."

Adam chuckled. "I'll be retired before she's out of high school."

Adam was so vital and fit that she never thought about him retiring. But he'd turned fifty-four in June and Kate was only three. She didn't want him to work into his seventies unless he truly loved what he was doing—and that he would leave the more dangerous work to his younger staff. Not that she wanted her kids in danger-ous work, either, but they had that thrill-seeker and protector gene for sure.

"But I want them all to choose their own paths," Adam contin-ued. "Not be forced into anything."

"I wonder how Ryder and Megan are doing with the kids," she asked. They were rarely out of her care and oversight and then usually Adam took over.

"I went out on the porch before turning in and heard lots of giggling. Someone was making shadow animals against the wall of the tent."

"Probably Ryder. Man, it's good to see him so relaxed, although he seems to be able to handle being around people better every day."

"Mm-hmm." Thoughts turned to the conversation she'd had with Megan when they'd visited the ranch earlier this summer. "They'll make great parents."

"Too bad they can't have kids of their own, but let's hope something works out for them when they're ready to adopt."

"Definitely."

Karla's hand drifted lower across his abs. The man hadn't lost his firm physique despite it being a few years since he'd retired from the Marine Corps. He didn't work out to obsession, but performed a daily regimen of exercises in their home gym to stay in shape. She'd started working out, too, although they couldn't work out together.

When she reached inside his shorts to take his cock in hand, his entire body stiffened.

He took her hand and removed it. "Feels good, Kitten, but nothing's going to happen with my mom across the hall."

It had been a couple days since they'd made love, what with all they'd had to do to get ready for the trip. "I've missed you, Sir. Surely you can come quietly." How many times had he made her do that?

"Don't be a brat." His hand reached for her nipple and pinched it. "But I've missed touching you like this too." When he pinched her harder, she gasped, then smiled.

"How far do you think we can go without being heard?"

"I'd say that depends on you. I don't make much noise myself."

Pfft. She wondered how much this bed would squeak when he pounded into her.

"Sir, I don't expect the kids to make it through the night out there and if they don't, they probably won't go back in that tent the rest of the week. If we're going to do anything this week, we'd better get to it tonight."

Besides, everyone in the house was an adult.

"Better lock the door to give us some advanced warning in case we're interrupted."

Karla left the bed, crossed the room, and locked the bedroom door. The door to the patio had never been unlocked, so that should be fine. She returned to stand beside the bed and slowly shimmied her nightie over her head, undulating her hips like a harem-girl. She tossed the gown to the floor as Adam shucked his shorts, his erection standing tall and proud.

Nearly an hour later, Karla's heart continued to beat fast as she slowly returned to earth from her excruciatingly quiet orgasm. She rested her head against his shoulder again and closed her eyes. Despite the urgency to finish before being interrupted, Adam had taken his time to keep her from exploding until she was at the brink of screaming her head off.

"That was incredible." Her chest rose and fell as she continued to catch her breath. Kink was great, but sometimes just making love was all she needed and wanted.

"You did great at keeping the decibel levels low, Kitten. Doubt anyone heard us."

"I don't care if they did. We're adults and married to boot, although I'm sure your mother knows all of her kids had sex before marriage."

"No doubt. She's no prude."

"I love her a lot. Glad she's able to be a part of this week. Patrick did a great job at fixing the place up with her accessible bathroom and the changes to the kitchen, not to mention ramps to the front door and from our patio here as a backup in an emergency. I enjoyed prepping dinner with her and Marge. Glad they took charge, though. Megan and I just followed orders, although I know Megan can cook better than I can."

"You're a great cook. I don't remember going hungry or sending anything you've made me back to the kitchen."

"You're just being supportive."

"Fishing for a compliment, Kitten?"

She grinned. "Maybe." He smacked her bare ass, making it sting. "What?" She propped herself up on her elbow and blinked her eyes at him innocently.

"We're going to have to work on that. Stop comparing yourself to others. You're all I've ever wanted or needed. And you're the best mother our kids could have. We're all going to love you whether you can cook fancy meals or not. Besides, you're trying to get your singing career off the ground, and that takes up what little time you have left after taking care of the kids."

Karla smiled down at him. "Thank you, Adam." She kissed him lightly. "And thanks for being supportive of my career. I love that you've been taking time off work to take care of the kids when I'm recording or otherwise occupied with my own work."

"The kids are both our responsibilities. Besides, it's good for them to see how a daddy is supposed to act." A cloud shadowed his eyes momentarily. He hadn't had that experience with his own father. "I want to be a part of their lives and my agency will never take precedence over my family—ever."

She laid her head on his chest, feeling his heart beating against her cheek. "I'm so lucky to have you."

"Not as lucky as I am, Kitten. I never expected to find someone I could love as much as you—and sure as hell never expected to have one, much less three, children at my age."

She thumped him on the arm. "Oh, stop. Age is just a number. Be grateful that you're at a point in your life where you own your own business and can make family a priority. Non-career military types usually can't leave their nine-to-five jobs or working twelve-hour shifts until at least sixty-five."

He'd often told her how many regrets he had that his years on active duty and during deployments hadn't given him the luxury of spending more time with Joni before she got cancer.

"Not sure I've been doing that enough lately, though, hon. With this arsonist running around, things have exploded with more cases than my team can keep up with. As soon as I bring the new hires up to speed, I'll be able to delegate more. Then I'll be able to spend more time with you and the kids."

She patted him on his bare chest. "I'm just glad you were able to get away this week."

"We have Damián and Grant to thank for helping to hold down the fort for me."

"Whatever it takes. I'm sure they're loving it, especially Grant." That woman always seemed to be itching for a fight or to go after the bad guys on any shore. "I know life won't stay this busy for us forever, but once our new careers are established, we'll make everything work. At least our kids aren't wanting for anything, and they have all the love we can give them."

*   *   *

Megan

"Go fish!" Pax told Rori with great glee. Megan shook her head. He so loved besting her at something. The two were so competitive.

Cozy inside their tent, Ryder and the kids played cards. Earlier, she and Ryder had devoured the s'mores they'd made on a small cookstove outside their tent. But the triplets chose to eat the marshmallows, graham crackers, and Hershey bars separately and not cooked. At least their way was slightly less messy.

"Do you have any fours?" Kate asked Megan.

"Sorry, honey. You'll have to go fish." She hoped one of the kids won the game. She'd feel guilty if she or Ryder beat them at cards or any other game. Did Karla and Adam let them win? She wasn't quite sure how to throw a game of Go Fish.

Ten minutes later, Kate played the winning pair to the groans of Pax and Rori.

"Who wants to hear a spooky story?" Ryder asked to get them excited again.

A chorus of "Me! ME! MEEE!" went up with hands raised and waving in the air. Too bad they hadn't been able to have a campfire, but the area was dry and fires were prohibited here this summer.

Kate scrunched her brows together. "It won't be too scary, will it?"

Ryder shook his head. "Not too much, and it's just a story, not real.

Kate nodded, but scrambled up next to Megan, who wrapped her arms around her and settled her into the empty space between her legs.

"Okay, let's all scoot in closer," Ryder suggested as he pulled the other two into their cozy circle. "Once upon a time, long, long ago," Ryder began, "a couple was riding home in their carriage and—"

"What's a carriage?" Rori asked.

"It's like Cinderella's coach," Megan explained.

Kate's eyes opened wide. "Ohh!"

"Pretty!" Rori agreed.

Megan smiled at the image that must be running through their minds of a pumpkin-shaped coach but gave Ryder the nod to continue.

"When it got dark—they didn't have streetlights in those days— they decided they would have to stop and stay at the next house they came upon."

"Who's dwiving the coach," Pax asked.

Ryder didn't seem to have an answer, and Megan couldn't really help him with this one. Someone would have to drive the coach.

"You know what?" Ryder asked. "I don't think it was a carriage, after all. It was a buckboard like they used to ride it around here."

Good save.

"Anyway, soon they saw a house just off the road that was surrounded by lots of trees. When they knocked, an old couple answered the door and invited them inside to share their supper."

"What about their horse?" Kate asked.

"Oh, the old couple let them feed the horse some hay and gave him a stall in their barn." Ryder improvised nicely. Apparently, the devil was in the details with spooky stories for toddlers.

"That was nice of them," Kate said.

"Yes, it was," Megan commented. "People were more trusting of strangers back then."

"Now the traveling man offered to pay the old couple for taking care of them and their horse, but the couple wouldn't hear of it. So everyone went to sleep. The next morning, the travelers packed up early to leave so they wouldn't impose on the couple anymore. And his wife left a shiny silver dollar on the table before they tiptoed out to finish their journey home."

He had them enthralled now, because no one interrupted to ask any more questions, no doubt waiting for the spooky part to be revealed.

"When the couple reached the next town, they stopped at a tavern to have lunch and told their server about the old couple." Ryder leaned in for dramatic effect. "The server looked like she'd seen a ghost. 'Where was this house?' The travelers told her exactly where the house had been, and the server shook her head. 'No, that's impossible. The old couple's house burned down five years ago, and they didn't make it out alive.'"

"Ghosts! Ghosts!" Pax shouted, jumping to the punchline, and his sisters huddled closer against Ryder and Megan.

"Well, tell you the truth, the travelers didn't believe her," Ryder continued, not saying one way or another if Pax had guessed correctly. "The tavern server asked if she could leave work to go back with the travelers and make sure they were talking about the same place. She directed them to the same spot where the travelers had stayed the night, walked into the trees, and…"—Ryder paused for effect—"they saw a burnt-out house from a fire that must have happened years ago. *Five* years, to be exact."

Ryder lowered his voice. "All the man recognized from the night before was the sturdy table. Then his wife screamed and pointed at the table. Sitting on the top of the soot-blacken table was a shiny silver dollar."

"Pax right!" Rori shouted. "Ghosts! Like Casper!"

In an effort to salvage their campout without sending the kids to their mom and dad's room, Megan pulled out a sweet bedtime story that she hoped would erase the terror of the ill-delivered ghost story. They probably should have thought this through better. Ryder assured her it was great fun when someone played the trick on him and his friend who lived in the Jemez Pueblo, but they were probably teens at the time.

"Pax, come sit on my lap too," she coaxed, and he did so. Ryder and Rori moved closer so they could see the pictures in the book with the camp flashlight filling the tent with light. After finishing the story, and another, their little eyes seemed to be drooping somewhat.

"Okay, time for us to snuggle into our sleeping bags." The kids scrambled out of their laps and she and Ryder rolled out the three bags. The triplets crawled inside the one between hers and Ryder's, all snuggling in together. After almost half an hour of good-nights and *Why* or *How come* questions about the stories they'd told, Megan thought they'd finally drifted off to sleep when Pax said, "Aunt Megan, are ghosts weal?"

"What do you think?"

"I never seen one."

"Most people never do, so it's hard to say what's real and what isn't." Was that judicious enough not to keep the boy up all night? "But that was a made-up story just to have fun tonight. There's nothing to be afraid of, honey," she assured him, tousling his hair. "Ryder and I are here with you three, and everything's fine."

Maybe it was a good thing she and Ryder didn't have kids of their own. They sure had a lot to learn about child development and what kids could handle at what ages.

"Can I sweep in your bag, Aunt Megan?"

While he was already right next to her, she opened the bag so he could crawl inside with her. Sniffling, he curled up next to her. The little boy's hair smelled like baby shampoo and sunshine.

Tears came to Megan's eyes as she thought about what could've been if only she hadn't made that fateful decision.

*   *   *

Ryder

Ryder sure had a lot to learn about kids! Ryder breathed a sigh of relief that the five occupants of this tent finally seemed to be settling down, thanks to Megan's idea to read them a story about fuzzy bunnies.

The kids at the ranch were usually older and often under parental or adult supervision from someone else most of the time.

Megan's sniffle from across the tent caught his attention. She lay curled up in her sack with Pax. Was the close proximity making her think about having kids of their own again? While Ryder hadn't been enthusiastic about becoming parents earlier, he wanted Megan to be happy, and if that meant they should adopt sooner rather than later, they would make it work.

"Red?" he whispered, hoping not to wake anyone. "Are you okay?"

She remained silent for the longest time, and he thought she wasn't going to admit to being awake and crying, but at last she responded in a soft voice without turning around. "Yes. Too much on my mind to sleep."

Ryder smiled at her trying to hide her emotions from him. She'd probably be all right tonight, but they'd have to talk about this when they were alone again. He'd do whatever it took to give her a child of her own to raise, if that was even what the problem was. He hoped it wasn't anything he couldn't make happen for her.

The two remained silent for a few minutes. He wished she was within arm's length and he would stroke her arm and back to comfort her. After a while, her breathing became steady, so he figured she'd fallen asleep.

He didn't succumb to slumber as quickly. Thoughts about how they would go about adopting ran through his head. He liked to have a plan for things rather than just let them take their course. But he didn't know anyone who'd adopted before. He'd better look into the possibilities online when they got home. Pulling his phone out here in the tent might wake up the kids.

Megan was twelve years younger than he was; Ryder had turned forty-one last month. Would agencies even let someone his age adopt a kid? Of course, they could ask for an older child. He'd heard people got faster placements in those cases than with babies. He'd talk more about it to Megan—

"Unca Ryder?" Sounded like Kate.

"Yes, baby?" Apparently, he wasn't the only one wide awake tonight.

"Why doesn't anyone believe Whiskey's my horse?" *Yes, definitely Kate.*

It wasn't Ryder's place to speak to a kid about things like this, so he'd better play it safe. "I'm not sure, honey." He paused a minute to gather his thoughts. "That's something you should talk with Mommy and Daddy about."

"They said don't talk about him anymore."

Poor kid. While Ryder had no explanation for why Kate insisted she'd lived in this cabin before and that Whiskey was her horse, what could he say to her?

"Um, Kate, sweetie, are you sure you didn't overhear one of the grownups talking about the horse before?"

"No." She remained silent a moment. "You don't believe me too?"

He would let her talk, at least. "What do you remember about Whiskey?" he whispered, hoping they wouldn't wake the others in the tent.

After a short time, she said, "I can remember riding in a coach like Cinderella's."

A coach or a stagecoach? Kate wouldn't remember anything earlier than the past year, would she? He wasn't aware of Karla and Adam taking them on a stagecoach ride. Curious, he wanted to know more.

"What was that like?"

"Bumpy. Dirty I was scared."

"What were you afraid of?"

"The scary-looking man with me. But it was just Johnny. And he wasn't scary like the other man."

"The other man in the coach?"

"No. I was going to his place. But then it burned down, just like the house in your story."

What the hell? Ryder definitely needed to talk to Adam.

"Why don't we get some sleep tonight, Kate? We'll talk about this with Daddy in the morning."

"I can't tell him. Daddy doesn't believe me."

Ryder wasn't sure what he believed at this point, either, but needed to stay neutral. "Maybe if he hears more of the story that you remember…" He'd what? Well, at the very least, Adam might know where she'd learned about stagecoaches and bad guys.

"Go too, Unca Ryder?"

"Sure. I'll be there." In some ways, he'd rather not be, but in others, he couldn't wait to hear how Adam explained all this. While he'd been exposed to a culture that believed in things that were mystical and spiritual, he hadn't experienced much of that himself, except during the sweat lodge ceremony. And there were extenuating circumstances that time.

*   *   *

Adam

After breakfast, while Marge and Megan cleared the dishes and Karla cleaned up the mess the kids had made, Ryder came to Adam when he was in conversation with Patrick and said, "I think Kate needs to tell you something. It's pretty serious."

What on earth could a three-year-old have to say that was so serious? He glanced across the room and saw Kate staring up at the portrait over the fireplace again, almost as if in silent communication with Adam's great-great-grandparents. He didn't understand her fascination with the painting. Must be because she wanted a horse so badly. That wasn't going to happen, although she had her pick of horses when she got a little bigger and they visited the Dreams Found Ranch.

Of course, the portrait had been special to him too growing up; he'd heard stories about Kate and Johnny his whole life. Maybe he'd stared at the portrait the same way. He'd been told stories about Kate and Johnny from a very young age. They'd also been the parents of multiples—two sets of twins. Must be they ran in the family.

Adam had planned to tell his kids the stories about them one night this week, but they'd spent their first night in Megan and Ryder's tent.

"Why don't we go outside?" Adam suggested to Ryder as he excused himself from his brother.

Across the room, he called out to Kate. "Uncle Ryder says you want to talk to me about something, Kate."

She turned and nodded, her face solemn with a touch of worry. "I wanna talk about her." Kate pointed up at the portrait.

Maybe now they would get to the bottom of whatever it was she'd overheard.

"Why don't we go for a walk, hon?"

"Me too, Daddy!" Rori cried out.

"I'll take you on the next walk, just the two of us. And Pax will get his turn too."

Rori's lower lip jutted out, but the three kids didn't always have to do everything together. The pediatrician had told them long ago it was good for each to get to spend special time alone with each parent during this trip.

Crossing the room to take Kate by the hand, Adam gave Ryder a nod, and they walked toward the door. Outside, Adam chose their path along the ridgeline and began to walk in silence.

Kate scrutinized the surrounding scenery as they moseyed at the toddler's pace. Kate spoke first. "Everything looks different."

She'd never been here before, but he decided to humor her. "How so, Kate?"

"Trees all gone."

Adam glanced around. There seemed to be plenty of trees by his estimation. He decided to let that go. "What is it you wanted to talk with me about, Kate?"

She looked up at Ryder first, who smiled reassuringly to her, then she turned to Adam.

"I remember when I was Kate."

Adam grinned. "You're still Kate, aren't you?"

She shook her head, sending her curls flying. "No, I mean when I was the Kate in the picture."

Here we go again. The kid sure had a vivid imagination.

"Tell me more about when you were Kate."

"We had a bumpy coach ride. And Johnny saved me from the big fire. And my horse Whiskey."

Adam stopped in his tracks and zeroed in on Ryder. Had he been feeding her stories last night? Pax had been going on and on at breakfast about a ghost story. Perhaps Megan had shared them with him, so he definitely could know more about the original Kate than he was letting on.

But Ryder shrugged and shook his head, looking as surprised as

Adam. "Kate told me about all that last night too," Ryder said. "I figured you'd be able to explain those stories to her."

Adam's mom had told her family story about Kate traveling from Boston via train to work in a theater as a seamstress and how she'd traveled by stagecoach the last miles to Deadwood back in 1879 only to fall prey to the unscrupulous Al Swearingen and his theater that was actually a brothel.

His little Kate didn't watch Westerns on TV and hadn't ridden in a stagecoach at any time in her life, so she couldn't possibly know these details. Someone must have told her the stories.

However, her mention of Johnny Montague rescuing her from the fire gave him the most pause. Kate had almost been killed in one of the fires that burned down the Swearingen's Gem *Theater*.

Could Joni be having a little fun with him again from the Great Beyond? Adam wasn't about to talk to a three-year-old about the spirit of his dead first wife coming back to put silly notions in her head.

But he couldn't just leave the conversation hanging in the air like this now, could he?

Curious, he decided to ask her a few more questions.

"What else do you remember?"

"Johnny built that cabin." Kate pointed to the cabin where the family was staying this week. Of course, it has changed over the years, but the center rooms had originally made up the entire cabin.

And yet, Adam needed to know more. "Did you and Johnny move here before the fire?" Maybe he could trip her up in her facts.

"No, Daddy." She rolled her eyes. How'd she learn to do that? The kid was growing up too fast. "Fire happened first. Bad man wanted to hurt me. Johnny saved me."

While he didn't know much about that part of the story, hearing little Kate talk about it sent chills through Adam's body. Mom had never elaborated on what kind of danger Kate had been in other than the fire. More curious than ever, he couldn't wait to have a talk with his mother to fill in the missing pieces.

In some ways, he'd assumed most of the Kate and Johnny story had been fabricated to entertain him as a kid while camping out here after Dad lost yet another job. Maybe there was some truth to it, though.

Some tourism brochures he looked at said there was a research center in town. Adam might want to spend some time there while up here this week. Had Kate and Johnny's story made the local papers and had any survived all these years?

Right now, though, he needed to address the problem at hand.

Joni, leave my kid alone. Life's hard enough without having people make fun of you for saying weird shit like this.

Adam almost expected to hear Joni give some wise-ass remark but heard nothing. He sighed, almost afraid to ask any more questions. "That sounds like an interesting story." He thought a minute and added, "Remember anything else?"

"Whiskey ran really fast. Johnny didn't like me to ride fast. But Whiskey loved me. Whiskey wouldn't hurt me."

That was a tidbit that hadn't been passed down through the family lore, making Adam even more certain Joni had to be feeding Kate information. As fascinating as the stories might be to her, Adam needed to find some distractions for Kate this week to get her mind solidly back in the present.

"Let's see what kinds of animal signs we can find on our walk. Ryder, you're good at tracking, aren't you?"

Ryder grinned. "Sure am. My friend Carlos and I used to track all the time."

The three of them continued along the path until it no longer resembled one, but Kate was a trouper and trudged along single file between Adam and Ryder into the woods.

"Look at this, Kate." Ryder pointed to a hole in the ground. "That's where a snake lives."

Kate screamed and practically climbed Adam as if he were a

tree to get away. "Don't let it get me, Daddy!" She burrowed her face against his neck.

"Don't be afraid, kiddo" Ryder assured her. "Most of the time, if you don't threaten them, they won't bother you. I'll bet this snake isn't even in its hole. Probably out looking for mice to eat."

"Eww. I don't like mice too!"

Adam wondered which she liked the least. It was a toss-up for him.

"You know, I have a stronger connection to the snake than most," Ryder went on, attempting damage control. "The snake is my spirit animal."

What the fuck did he just say? Adam shot Ryder a skeptical look.

Here they were diving right back into the woo-woo shithole.

"What's a spirit animal?" Kate asked him.

Ryder gave Adam a belated look of apology. "Sorry, Top. I probably shouldn't have brought that up." He must really be rattled, because he hadn't called Adam Top in years.

But you're damned right you shouldn't have. Way to have my six.

"Go on," Adam coaxed. This he had to hear.

"Well, I went on a vision quest and learned…" He must have noticed both of their confused expressions. "You see, in some Native American cultures, people believe that a certain animal watches out for them their whole life. I went on a quest for four days and nights to discover what mine was—and it turned out to be the snake."

"What's mine?"

"Kiddo, it can take many, many years to find out what yours is. But start paying attention to the animals around you, the ones you dream about, the ones—"

"Horses!" She bounced up and down in Adam's arms. "I dream about horses!"

And very vividly, at that.

Adam didn't believe in spirit animals, either, but hearing that

Kate had been dreaming of horses just led to the most logical explanation for her attaching herself to Whiskey.

And if he talked with Mom, Megan, and Patrick, he'd probably figure out who had told her the horse's name.

There. Mystery solved.

Section Six

Angelina

Angelina couldn't believe that all three founding Doms plus Luke had managed to be at the Masters at Arms Club with their submissives at the same time. It had been more than two years since they'd been here together for Angelina's bridal shower.

She and Marc, on the other hand, came in every now and then, because they didn't have kids to worry about yet—only their demanding careers.

The four couples arrived well after dark to make Ryder and Megan's job of babysitting the five kids easier. At one point, Karla had invited them to join in, too, but Megan had laughed, saying it would be too weird to go to a kink club with her brother. At least as far as playing. They had joined in the Alive Day commemoration for Damián and Marc nearly three years ago.

After parking around the corner, because on a Friday night there hadn't been any spots closer to the club, they heard the throbbing beat of the music pouring out of the great room the moment they opened the door. Specimen's "Kiss Kiss Bang Bang"? Mistress Grant must be in charge of the playlist. Angelina smiled. The Domme and Damián had always steered toward that type of gritty sound.

She and Marc greeted a long-time member of the club at the reception desk then made their way down the entry hall. Inside the great room, she couldn't believe how packed the place was compared to the Wednesday night they'd been here in June.

Mistress Grant, dressed in leather from her shoulders to her boots, spotted the group, smiled, and crossed the room to greet them.

"So glad you could make it! I wasn't sure if something might have come up with one of the kids."

"We just wanted to wait until they were sound asleep," Adam said. "All was quiet when we left the house."

"You sure have things hopping tonight," Damián said as he glanced around the room. "I see a few familiar faces, but it looks like you've expanded the membership."

Mistress Grant nodded and *almost* smiled, apparently pleased that he'd notice. "Most are members, although we do have a few kink-curious guests tonight. I'm keeping a close eye on them, of course, as are the dungeon monitors." Both glanced at Angelina, no doubt remembering the first time she'd been brought here as a guest and what a disaster that had been.

She shuddered, and Marc stroked her back to reassure her that nothing like that would happen again.

"We don't want to keep you," Marc said to Mistress Grant, "but perhaps later tonight we can have a drink and catch up."

"Sounds great. Things tend to wind down shortly after midnight." She turned toward Luke. "Are you and Adam still interested in doing the dual suspension demo tonight?"

Luke glanced down at Cassie who nodded almost imperceptibly. That she'd agreed to do something in public amazed Angelina, given how new she was to kink. Even though Angelina wasn't new to the club or kink, she didn't think she'd want to be doing that demo or any other. She and Marc were happy with their bedroom kink and the rare visit to Gunnar's home, although they had commissioned Luke to make them furniture for their own playroom now that life was settling down a bit for them.

"Yes, ma'am," Luke answered the Domme.

"It'll take us some time to set up," Adam began, "so maybe we'll do it in an hour or so, if that works for you." Seeing him defer to the new owner seemed odd, but the torch had definitely been passed.

"That's perfect. Several people are here tonight mainly to see the demo." She smiled at Adam. "You've been missed, my friend."

He shook his head and smiled. "I don't miss the amount of work it takes to run this place. But I do miss doing demos and hanging out with the members."

"I promise not to put you to work, so stop by anytime. Now, what can I get you and your subs to drink?"

"Just water for Kitten and me, please." He'd used Karla's submissive name, so Angelina made a mental note to get her mind into her submissive role too.

Master Adam—titles being one way to achieve that—rarely drank alcohol, and because he and Luke were doing a demo, Luke had also sworn off liquor tonight, making them the designated drivers. Like Master Adam, Marc always insisted that there be no alcohol consumed before scening. So first things first—playtime.

After Master Damián asked which theme room they'd been assigned to, he took Savannah by the hand and led her to the hallway.

"If you'll excuse us too," Master Marc said to Mistress Grant, "I've reserved the impact room for the next hour or so."

"Everything is set up as you requested," Grant assured him.

"Thanks, Grant."

"Oh, Sir, can I have a few minutes with Mistress Grant first?"

Master Marc lifted an eyebrow, but nodded. "You know where I'll be when you're ready, *cara*." He turned to Master Adam. "Don't start the demo until we come back out. I'm anxious to see what you and Luke are going to do tonight."

"Will do. Now, if you'll excuse us, I see some old friends I'd like to say hi to."

Master Adam took Karla's elbow, and Angelina waited until the three were out of hearing range before turning to the imposing Domme.

"I won't keep you, but I wanted to thank you for taking such good care of my friend Rico on his first time here last month. Whoever you paired him with did an excellent job of introducing him to kink."

"That's what I'm here for. Did he mention who that Dom was?"

Angelina shook her head. "Not a peep, although I'll admit I did try to find out. You'll be pleased to know he's taking the confidentiality rules very seriously."

Mistress Grant gave an enigmatic smile. "Good to hear."

When she didn't say anything more, Angelina figured she wouldn't find out who this mystery Dom was from Mistress Grant, either. "I guess I'd better join my Dom before he gets impatient. That never bodes well for my ass."

Mistress Grant smiled, but didn't say anything. As Angelina turned away, she shifted her focus to what was to come. Her entire body tingled with anticipation for her scene with Master Marc tonight. They'd been able to play more often at home now that he was no longer taking paramedic classes and things at her restaurant were running smoothly.

A frisson of electricity ran through the club, contagious to those present. Such a wide variety of dynamics and opportunities to try new things.

She couldn't wait to find out what Master Marc had in store for her tonight. He'd packed his long floggers, so at some point, she hoped he'd do his Florentine session of rhythmic flogging. Her back and ass tingled in anticipation.

* * *

Cassie

As they stood next to their husbands, Cassie wasn't sure why she had agreed to this. Cassie had only been in here once before, for Angelina's private bridal shower more than two years ago. Needless to say, that visit had been much tamer than tonight would be. Tonight's atmosphere made her a little uncomfortable.

Kitty touched the beautiful necklace she'd worn since returning from her honeymoon. The one she never took off.

"Sir, should I have worn my leather one tonight?" Kitty asked Adam.

Her leather *what?* Necklace?

Adam grinned at her. "If you remember your place and protocols, Kitten, you can wear your day collar throughout. But I brought your play one in case you need a reminder."

Collar? Cassie's gaze zoomed back in on the Black Hills gold necklace, and she came to the realization it had never been a necklace at all. Kitty had been collared by Adam on their honeymoon!

She'd always thought a BDSM collar was a leather one and looked like a dog's collar. Never in a million years would she have guessed this was Kitty's collar. Did other submissives wear them too?

She hadn't noticed one on Angelina, but now that she thought of it, Savannah always wore the same platinum necklace. Was she collared too?

When Kitty referred to him as Master Adam, did this mean she was his slave?

How did I not know about this?

Cassie glanced toward Luke, who didn't seem shaken by Adam's words at all. Did he know? Is this something he'd one day want her to do too?

"Adam, why don't we check out the rigging and get started?"

Luke asked.

Not wanting Luke to pull out a collar for her, she decided to remember her protocols tonight, just in case.

"Sounds good to me."

Luke and Adam placed pillows on the floor in front of each of them to kneel on while they waited. Luke kissed Cassie on the cheek before helping her into position. They'd talked about this being part of the deal tonight, and she'd been fine with it before concerns about how deeply into the lifestyle he would want to take her crept up.

But Luke had always assured her their relationship would be negotiated and wouldn't involve anything she wasn't willing to do. He'd always respected her and her opinion, so she decided not to let this bother her. She and Luke would talk tonight and on the drive home.

With her friend settled on her knees beside her as well, the two Doms walked toward the stage. Luke pulled from his bag a number of bundles of hemp rope of assorted muted colors, while she and Kitty waited for their part in the demo to begin.

While she and Luke had been experimenting with new types of bondage and rope play, some of which he had told her would be used tonight, their activities had been mild compared to what she imagined must take place in this club.

"What have we gotten ourselves into, Kitty?"

Kitty took Cassie's hand and squeezed it. "Girl, your hand is like ice!" She rubbed her hands over Cassie's to infuse warmth into it. "I know we've never played in public before, but you said you and Luke have been practicing rope suspension, right?"

Cassie nodded.

"Luke and Adam will take very good care of us."

"I know." She should count her blessings. "At least they are letting us keep our panties on." Her face grew warm even talking with Kitty about something like this. Cassie was not sure she was cut out for what was about to happen. She had never been comfortable displaying herself to others. It had taken a long time to even be comfortable with her husband.

Kitty giggled. "I'll admit, with so many new people here tonight, I'm grateful for that concession too!" She leaned in closer. "Adam even told me I could wear a tube top if I wanted, given all my tits have been through in the past few years, but I have a bit of an exhibitionist streak and decided to be daring. Besides, it will make it easier for Adam to play with them."

Cassie's face grew warm. Would Luke feel left out if he didn't have free access to hers too? Luke had succeeded in convincing Cassie that what he and Adam planned to do would be much more sensual for her if she did not wear a bra. Under her blouse, however, she did wear a tube top she had borrowed from Kitty. She hoped Luke did not plan to bare her breasts.

Glancing around the room at the couples, sometimes trios, in various states of kinky dress and paraphernalia who mingled at tables or at the bar, Cassie tried to imagine how vanilla she must look in her wraparound skirt and blouse. Kitty wore a similar skirt, probably in solidarity.

Cassie's focus returned to the stage where Luke and Adam prepared the rope they would use. She did not see any furniture like what Luke usually made, but perhaps that was primarily for home use.

When Luke turned to her and smiled, her breath caught in her throat. Not in fear, but excitement. Was it time? He started toward where she and Kitty waited, and Cassie held her breath.

"How are you doin', Sweet Pea?" Luke cupped her cheek, and she let go of Kitty's hand, letting her husband comfort her instead.

"Fine, Luke"—her eyes opened wider—"I mean, *Sir.*" She glanced down at his boots. He had talked to her about the protocols used in the club and how a submissive should address her Dom in a setting like this. At home, they rarely used protocols. Her head had been spinning all week trying to remember everything.

Luke chuckled and tucked a finger under her chin until she met his gaze. "You'll do great, darlin'. Most important thing is—don't forget to breathe."

Something else she had momentarily forgotten how to do. Would she do anything right tonight?

He kissed her on the cheek again, took her hand in his and helped her to her feet. Luke whispered, "I can't wait to show off my beautiful rope bunny."

His words warmed her heart—well, that part about her being beautiful, not the showing her off part.

Adam took Kitty's hand as well and led her to the center of the stage, while Luke and Cassie remained on the sidelines.

Luke leaned closer to her. "Master Adam's going to take things a little slower for the audience, but I want to tie you without too much distracting you. Once he gives us the go-ahead, we'll do similar ties for you."

Fortunately, the crowd was quiet and respectful. She did not have to be concerned about anyone getting out of hand or threatening her. Between Mistress Grant and her helpers—Luke called them *dungeon monitors*—it appeared that the club's submissives were safe to explore without being hit on or harassed by anyone. And of course, Luke and Adam would be watching over her and Kitty so that nothing went wrong.

And yet, she had to keep reminding herself of that.

Adam—*Master Adam*—told Kitty to remove her blouse. Again, Cassie hoped she'd be able to keep on most of her clothes, but might that be about to change.

Cassie glanced up and noticed only a single hook on the ceiling. Would they suspend Kitty first then her? She'd hoped Luke would let her get it over with first, but this was a demo, and she supposed it also needed to be a teaching moment.

Master Adam told the audience he'd be using a TK tie, but as she watched it being tied, she recognized it as what Luke called the box tie. Cassie liked this one. Even though it wasn't as decorative as the ties Luke normally did, it was comfortable, and she had a little bit of room to flex her hands if she needed to.

Thank the goddess.

While Adam explained to the audience what he was doing as he applied Kitty's chest harness, Cassie closed her eyes to tune out everything except for the litany of instructions and protocols in her head and Luke's solid presence beside her. Her breathing slowed again.

Cassie's body tingled as she anticipated the rope rubbing against her almost bare breasts.

I hope Luke doesn't ask me to remove more clothing than I'm comfortable with.

"All set, Luke."

Master Adam's words brought Cassie out of her head. She met Luke's gaze.

"That's our cue, Sweet Pea."

Her heart beat loudly as Luke led her to the center of the stage just as Adam lowered Kitty to her side on a cushioned mat.

"We'll be suspending Kitten and Sweet Pea from the same hard point," Master Adam explained to the audience. Using their nicknames seemed strange, but she supposed it was how it was done in the club scene.

Wait! What? Cassie stopped in her tracks and looked up at Luke again, silently asking if she'd heard correctly. They'd be suspended *together?*

He gave her a slight nod and stroked her lower back.

Before she had time to process that monumental information, Luke told her to remove her blouse. His commanding tone sent a shiver down her spine. With shaking fingers, Cassie undid the four buttons, slid the sleeves down her arms, and handed the blouse to Luke. He tossed it unceremoniously to the back of the stage, his eyes never leaving hers.

Trust me, Sweet Pea.

His eyes begged her to do so, and she did. Cool air washed over her skin, and her nipples peaked. Awareness of being watched crept into her thoughts, though, and her gaze flitted to the audience.

"Eyes on me, darlin'." She quickly did as he instructed, but he also shifted her body so that the audience was behind her.

Lucas always protects me.

He gave a nod to someone at Cassie's right, and the music switched from the frenetic tones they'd been hearing since arriving tonight to something much more soothing.

She relaxed even further. "Thank you, Sir."

"You know I'll make you as comfortable as I can, Sweet Pea." Luke glanced down at her breasts. "So beautiful." He cupped them through her tube top, and she dreaded that he might tell her to remove that as well. Instead, he bent to kiss each nipple in turn until the cloth became wet, which only caused the peaks to grow achingly larger.

Luke stood tall again and whispered, "Deep breath, Sweet Pea." His hands stroked her face, moved to her neck and shoulders, and down her arms. "That's it, darlin'. I want you totally relaxed for me."

Cassie focused only on his eyes, just as he had taught her to do at home. Everything and everyone around her faded away. The music and Luke's hands grounded her in the scene as she slowly breathed in and out.

Luke gave her a reassuring smile before stepping behind her and overlapping her forearms and hands to rest on the rise of her butt. Kitty lay on the mat in front of her, eyes closed, apparently getting into the zone for whatever was to come.

Cassie closed her eyes again, releasing any remaining tension from her body, and let her Dom apply the rope for her harness.

Don't think of anything but the rope. And Luke.

When he took her by the upper body and eased her onto the mat, she realized he'd completed her chest harness. Had she spaced out, or had he been incredibly fast doing so? Normally his ties took much longer.

He tied rope to her right ankle. "Now, Sweet Pea, rest your right foot against your left thigh as high above the knee as is comfortable." She bent her knee, which wasn't difficult since she was used to sitting in the lotus position for meditation. "I want you to tell me if you feel any discomfort or tingling in your leg."

"Yes, Sir."

The tug of the rope and the pressing of Luke's hand as he manipulated her leg the way he wished lulled her into the right headspace again.

"That's right, Sweet Pea. Keep your eyes closed. I want you to feel the rope, my presence, and nothing else."

She did exactly that as Luke wrapped, pulled, and twisted the rope and repositioned her leg and foot. Cassie relaxed her body, allowing him to easily manipulate her as he wished. The rope lulled Cassie into another realm where only she and Luke existed.

When he had finished with her right leg, he moved to her other one. She couldn't resist taking a peek from between her eyelashes. He'd tied a three-band *futomomo* on her right leg, and her foot's Achilles tendon was now snug against her upper thigh. On her left leg, however, he'd fashioned a simple thigh cuff, which took much less time. Nothing fancy, but no doubt both would be functional and safe.

Cassie assumed Kitty had been tied the same way, based on Luke's earlier comment, but she couldn't turn around to see. Besides, she wasn't supposed to open her eyes anyway. She hadn't truly opened them all the way just now, had she?

Would that be considered a bratty move in this lifestyle's protocols? Cassie grinned. She'd tell Kitty about her transgression later, but didn't want to confess it to Luke at the moment.

With her eyes completely closed again, she relaxed into the rope.

"Like that, Sweet Pea?"

Her smile grew wider. "It feels wonderful, Sir."

"Ready then?"

Ready? "For what? Sir!" she added the honorific title quickly.

He grinned. "You'll see. Just remember to let me know right away if you have any discomfort or numbness."

Cassie lost her concentration momentarily as she wondered how she'd be suspended with Kitty, but she quickly reined in those stray thoughts. That she'd be tied in tandem with her best friend suddenly pleased her. They were in this together, just as they'd done so many things together in college and in the years since.

Besides, on the positive side, everyone would be looking at Kitty and Adam; she would become invisible to all but Luke.

At least that's what I'm telling myself.

*   *   *

Luke

Luke smiled the moment Cassie's body totally surrendered to the rope. He hadn't expected her to relax so quickly while being watched by a couple dozen people, but ultimately, she'd managed to tune out the crowd and focus. He'd never been prouder to be her Dom and earn her trust in such a profound way.

Turning her away from the audience, in part to play with her privately, had the added bonus of helping her tune out distractions. Having Cassie keep her eyes closed now helped too. She wouldn't want to see all the faces staring at her anyway. Playing some of her favorite meditation music relaxed her too. Adam had okayed the playlist change, even if it wasn't necessarily his or Karla's taste.

That Adam wanted this experience to be good for Cassie reassured Luke he'd partnered with the right mentor.

Cassie had never scened with anyone but Luke before this. Even though Adam had to keep explaining things to the audience, Cassie seemed to have blocked him out too. Perhaps Luke's distracting her after he'd turned her back to the audience had helped. He loved any excuse to play with her breasts, but doing so in public had excited him more than he'd expected.

Would she reach subspace tonight?

I sure hope so.

He and Adam had decided not to let their rope bunnies know what all was in store for them until they were immersed in the scene, a strategy that seemed to be working.

Adam's level of expertise always intimidated and fascinated Luke, and he himself couldn't wait for the dramatic finale of the demonstration today. Despite all the practicing they'd done, having his mentor here to double check everything gave Luke even more confidence.

These ties were far simpler than the more decorative ones Luke usually tied at home, but Adam stressed safety when it came to suspension. And rightly so.

Luke couldn't wait to give Cassie the best suspension experience she'd ever had.

Adam hoisted Karla using the crucial red upline attached to the back of her TK harness, positioning her on her side facing out. Awaiting their turn, Luke stroked Cassie's neck, shoulders, and arms to help keep her centered and calm. For the most part, Cassie seemed to be excited about what was to come.

Karla appeared to be laser-focused on her Dom rather than the audience. No one loved rope more than Karla, although Cassie was growing to enjoy it more each time they played. Luke had been surprised when Adam told him this would be Karla's first time having someone else suspended with her, though. Once both were off the floor, he and Adam would be able to maneuver the two in any number of ways. Excitement built in Luke as well.

Adam secured the line, then handed a bundle of green-colored rope to Luke and stood back to watch him work with Cassie.

"Your turn, Sweet Pea."

Cassie smiled, eyes closed, and he returned the smile even if she couldn't see him. With Adam looking on, Luke followed the master's lead. He attached his first upline to the back of her TK chest harness and lifted Cassie off the ground until she was slightly higher than Karla. Horizontal and facing away from each other, the rope bunnies swayed slowly in the air like marionettes on a shared string. After securing that upline, Luke took a step back to admire his work, knowing Adam would have said something if Luke hadn't done it safely.

Luke leaned in to brushed Cassie's hair away from her face and noticed a grimace on her face. "Open your eyes for me, darlin'." She did so immediately and connected with him. "How are you doing?"

"Fine, Sir." Her words were forced.

Fine was sometimes Cassie's evasive response. "Be more specific, Sweet Pea."

"It's harder to fill my lungs now." She took a shallow breath. "But I'm not in any pain, Sir." Another breath. "Just trying to get used to the sensation."

"Hearing her call him *Sir* did his heart good. As you know, breathlessness is normal."

"Yes, Sir."

Confident she was okay at this point, he asked, "Ready to continue?"

Her sweet smile melted his heart. "Yes, Sir."

He lifted her chin and bent to place a kiss on her lips. "Good girl."

"You're doing great, Sweet Pea!" Karla's encouragement made her smile as well, and meant a lot to them both. "Just keep taking shallow breaths as often as you can."

Cassie nodded, then focused on Luke again, waiting.

"Sweet Pea, it's your choice as to whether you want to have your eyes open or closed. I'll leave that up to you."

"Thank you, Sir. I'm ready for more." With that, she promptly snapped her eyelids shut.

The cuff tie Adam had instructed him to use on Cassie's left thigh allowed her lower leg to dangle in the air, which didn't look as cool to him as the *futo*, but he did enjoy seeing her legs splayed open.

Luke wasn't ready to share his wife's hidden charms with the world, so he'd allowed her some modicum of modesty in her skimpy panties. That the girls had coordinated their underwear, both wearing pink, made him wonder how much the two of them had shared to prepare for tonight.

No doubt, everything.

Adam moved closer to Karla again and attached another upline to her thigh cuff, lifting her leg higher and tipping her body to put even more pressure on her chest. Karla groaned.

Not wanting to be left out of the fun, Luke did the same with Cassie's thigh cuff. Her groan brought a smile to his face as well, but he made sure she wasn't in any trouble. He caught Cassie opening her eyes at one point, but after seeing the audience, she closed them again quickly.

After giving the girls' bodies time to settle into those positions, it was time to shift them again.

The Doms moved in simultaneously to their bunnies and each took his own wife's *futo* and attached another green upline to the friction closest to each of their knees. On Adam's nod, Luke tugged on his line and positioned Cassie's leg high above her head.

"Ugh." Her moan as the chest pressure increased made him pause to check on her before tying her off.

"Breathe, Sweet Pea." He held the rope in place to allow her to express any issues or problems. When she didn't say anything, he asked, "Doing okay, darlin'?"

"Yes, Sir. Feels…amazing." She inhaled as deeply as she could. "Once I get used to this new position."

"I'll give you some time to do just that." Luke grinned as he secured the upline. He wouldn't be changing Cassie's position nearly as often after this as Adam would Karla's. Her friend had much more experience with rope suspension, although he would make sure Cassie had just as many mind-blowing moments tonight as Karla probably would.

Adam and Luke stepped back to make sure everything was to their liking. Adam moved in to make a small adjustment before giving Karla's knee a gentle push that set both women spinning a little faster.

"Oh!" Cassie's surprised reaction made Luke zoom in on her to make sure she was okay. When a huge smile broke out on her face, his Dom heart melted a little.

Luke became mesmerized by the glimpses of Cassie's satin pink undergarment peeking out. He heard several appreciative comments from those watching his wife and her best friend as they spun slowly, especially from the ladies in the crowd. The diaphanous skirts fluttered in the air, and judging by their wet panties, both were enjoying this demo as much as he and Adam were.

After a few more spins, and at Adam's signal, Luke stopped their motion with his wife's open legs spread in front of him. Karla faced the audience at the moment, just as Luke had planned it. They couldn't see Cassie or what he planned to do to her.

Luke leaned in and lowered the top edge of her tube top, which he'd been careful not to cover with the rope in the chest harness, and took one nipple into his mouth. He sucked it hard before giving it a nibble.

"Oh, yes, Luke!"

Her lapse in protocol signaled to him that she was as deeply into this scene, but here at the club, he needed to remind her of protocols.

"Sweet Pea, is that how you address your Dom?"

"Oh! I'm sorry, Sir!"

"That's my good girl." Not wanting to waste the moment, he brushed her skirt out of the way and his hand zeroed in on her panties. He slid his finger inside her underwear and then inside her pussy.

So wet.

"Whenever you're finished fooling around with your rope bunny, Luke," Adam hinted all too soon, "we can move on to the next part."

Busted. "I suppose I'll have to stop, Sweet Pea," he whispered, "but we'll continue later tonight when we're alone." She smiled as he pulled her top and panties back into place, and Luke gave Adam the nod.

"Now we're going to attach Kitten's *futo* to the front of Sweet Pea's TK harness," Adam told the audience.

Luke couldn't help but think that Adam's plan to tie Karla to a spot close to Cassie's heart was symbolic in so many ways. Their bond was a strong one, just like that rope would prove to be in a few minutes.

Luke moved in closer to watch, not that he intended to put Cassie through what Karla was about to experience. Cassie being such a novice, Adam agreed it wouldn't be wise to try something like that with her yet—and no way would Luke contradict his mentor.

Adam also assured him Karla would take the brunt of the shock-load maneuver. For Cassie, pressure on her chest harness would be the biggest effect. While Karla and Cassie might not agree about how much fun this was at first, Luke couldn't wait to see how the rest of this demo unfolded.

One thing he knew for certain—Cassie's responsiveness to the rope and his hands told him the possibilities were endless for them to play in the future.

*   *   *

Karla

Karla's body had begun to settle into this position, which only meant one thing. Master Adam would be shifting her weight again soon. She scanned the room trying to spot familiar faces in the audience to take her mind off the impending discomfort.

Marc and Angelina had returned from their scene room. So had Damián and Savannah. Mistress Grant watched from the bar area, because no one was ordering drinks at the moment. All eyes were on the stage. She'd missed being on stage at the club, although her performance tonight was quite different from when she'd performed here.

Master Adam, along with Luke, had outdone themselves in this dual suspension with her and Cassie. Showing off their rope skills—and making their bunnies feel cherished and a bit dizzy in the bargain—was delightful. She couldn't wait to compare notes with Cassie to see what she thought of it all. Her friend hadn't spoken her safeword, so it didn't sound as though she hated the experience in any way. Yet.

Perhaps Karla would become a mentor to her budding rope bunny friend.

As she swayed under the hook along with Cassie, a hand brushed her leg. Without warning, Master Adam grabbed the chest harness between her breasts with one hand and pinched her nipple with the other.

"Ready for more, Kitten?"

Tonight had been rather tame so far, partly because Adam had to explain everything to the audience. "Yes, Sir. Anything you'd like to do. I'm yours."

"Sweet music to my ears."

Adam tied her *futo* to the front of Cassie's TK harness, an awkward position to say the least.

"Now, it's time to scare my rope bunny a little," Adam announced to the audience.

Finally! Karla loved it when he caught her off guard.

"A word of caution. This is a move that should only be done by master riggers and with experienced bottoms."

Okay, that sounded more than a little ominous. Karla wasn't so much worried for herself, but what if they terrified Cassie into never wanting to do this again?

"Because Sweet Pea is fairly new to rope suspension," Master Adam continued, "she'll be an inert part of this shock load maneuver."

A what? Master Adam had never done anything like that to her before. She didn't remember the term, anyway. What on earth was her lovable Dom about to do to her—and how would it affect Cassie?

Karla tried to squirm around to face Master Adam, but he stood behind her. Then he stepped toward the audience, showing them something she couldn't see. The crowd gasped.

"Looks a little scary, doesn't it?" he asked them?

What on earth did he have in his hands?

When he finally turned toward her, and she saw the frightening implement, and her heart nearly exploded. The only way to describe it would be a *machete*.

"Time to cut one of our rope bunnies down." The way he stared at her and his earlier words made it clear Karla would be said bunny.

First, he turned back to the audience. "For all you Doms and Dommes who think you're hot stuff with rope, don't try anything like this without a master rigger on hand and a lot of experience. I won't be letting Luke and Sweet Pea do this, but I know Kitten will do just fine."

Karla wanted to argue that her experience was outdated and interrupted with pregnancy and mom time, but she trusted that he would take care of her and nothing bad would happen.

Master Adam moved closer, reached up with the hand not holding the machete to steady her again, then waited. "Deep breath, then brace yourself, Kitten."

Brace for what? Impact? Knifeplay?

Neither particularly thrilled her, although she reminded herself that Adam would do nothing to harm her. Without giving her any more time to worry further, Master Adam brought the heavy knife down in what must have been a swift whack at her last remaining upline—the red one. The movement happened in slow motion in her mind's eye, although judging by the whoosh of air emanating from his arm, it had to have been much faster.

Despite the upline being severed in two, it still seemed to take a second or two before the sensation of falling connected with her brain. With her hands bound behind her and her leg attached to Cassie's chest, she couldn't catch herself. Her head and torso hurtled toward the floor, and she squeezed her eyes shut when Adam made no attempt to catch her.

Karla screamed, "Good Lord! No!"

When Karla's body reached the point where it could fall no farther, the weight of her body yanked to a stop, and she dangled from her *futo*.

Ugh! Cassie's similar groan worried Karla. Was her friend in pain? Karla's entire weight hung from her friend's chest.

Shock load.

Now Karla understood what the term meant. Very aptly named, unlike some of the terms used in rope play. As Karla became used to the new position, she heard Cassie whisper, "Are you okay, Kitty?"

Thank goodness neither of them had passed out. "Yes. How about you?"

"I am, if you are."

No longer having to worry about her friend, Karla released the tension in her body. Her loose hair brushed the mat below them. The rush of blood to her head—combined with the tightening of the rope around her chest—made her dizzy. She couldn't fill her lungs. Her mind began to drift.

Karla drew as deep a breath as she could and closed her eyes.

She wasn't aware of anything else until a tug at the back of her hair brought her head up to see Master Adam's face. "How are you doing, Kitten?"

He didn't seem at all concerned judging by his grin. No doubt he'd had everything under control the whole time. But the least he could have done was prepare her.

"That machete scared ten years off my life." Despite her being slightly annoyed with him, a smile came to her lips. "But I can't wait to do this one again, Sir."

He gave her a hard, deep kiss, taking her breath away once again. "Glad you enjoyed it. Luke and I did too. And if I'm not mistaken, you and Sweet Pea both spent some time in subspace."

Had she? "How long have we been hanging?"

"I cut your upline about fifteen minutes ago."

"Wow!" No wonder she felt so mellow.

"But now it's time to get you both back down to Earth."

With her head barely a foot off the floor, she assumed she'd be lowered first.

"We'll attach a new upline to the back of your chest harness to lift you horizontally again before we lower you both to the floor."

Still a bit loopy from subspace, she simply nodded and closed her eyes, completely trusting her Dom. Everything happened quickly, and suddenly the weight of the rope decreased. She and Cassie couldn't see each other yet because their backs were to each other, so Karla closed her eyes again while the leg ropes were removed, followed by the TK harnesses.

When she was able to turn and face Cassie again, the glazed look in her friend's eyes made it apparent she had indeed reached subspace as well.

"That was amazing, Kitty."

"I have a feeling it won't be long before we find ourselves strung up again," Karla said with a laugh.

Adam and Luke said simultaneously, "No doubt about it, Kitten" and "You'd better believe it, Sweet Pea."

As the Doms removed the remaining ropes from their legs and massaged their muscles to restore blood flow, Karla's mind shifted to all the possibilities of what could happen in their playroom in the near future. Not to mention their bedroom!

*   *   *

Mistress Grant

Grant watched as the two couples wrapped up their scene on the stage. She'd made sure there were several bottles of water on stage for the Doms and subs once they were in the aftercare stage.

Why hadn't she studied rope work more? That hook and pulley system gave her some ideas, although she'd more likely just hogtie the sub—or subs. She always preferred inflicting pain and humiliation, especially with men, over anything as delicate and beautiful as decorative rope work. But suspension, on the other hand, had some possibilities.

Having Adam back in the club had certainly excited the membership. He'd been missed. Perhaps now that his kids weren't babies any longer, he and Karla would return more often.

Marisol had turned eleven this year. Grant remembered the wonderful times the two of them had had when she'd babysat, but that had been before she'd taken over running the club. Between this place and the various missions Gunnar sent her on, most of them short-term, but still time-consuming to prepare for, she wasn't around enough to see Marisol more often.

I need to make some time for her soon.

She wasn't sure how to take care of smaller kids, but Marisol would probably enjoy getting away to do things she couldn't do with a little brother under foot.

Luke stroked Cassie's arms as she sat cradled against his body in the aftercare stage of their scene. Grant hadn't spent a lot of time with them before, but had certainly come to appreciate the man's fine furniture and rigging equipment, like the one that he'd installed in theme room three earlier this month.

Marc and Angelina's presence tonight had presented a bit of a problem. Good thing Angelina's brother Franco had texted earlier to say he'd planned on coming to the club tonight. Grant had made it clear this would not be a good night for him to play here, although it had been a month since he'd stopped in and the twinks and malesubs missed him terribly.

When Franco had joined the club after moving to Denver almost two years ago, someone had let it slip the names of the original founders of the club, including Marc. Ever since, Franco had asked her to make sure he and his sister never crossed paths at the club no matter what. He hadn't come out to his family yet about being a Dom, much less that he preferred to play with men.

Because he'd become a regular on weekends, she'd warned him off. Of course, Marc and Angelina, who preferred a bedroom dynamic, usually went straight to one of the private theme rooms. Ironically, tonight it had been number eight, the same one where Franco had played recently. The siblings must have more in common than they otherwise thought. She could have easily steered Franco and whichever submissive he hooked up with to a different room tonight, but with the rope suspension demo planned, Grant rightly assumed that Marc and Angelina would want to be out here watching.

Franco's presence since last year had been bringing in a string of submissive gay men. Because Franco was unattached—and still was, she assumed—Grant loved to hook them up. Customer service, if you will.

Fuck that shit.

In some ways, though, the newer members felt more like hers than did the ones who'd joined under the founding Doms, and she wanted a hand in making sure their experience was rewarding so that they'd keep coming back to the club.

Grant's attention returned to the stage. Adam always knew how to get her off when she'd served as his bottom, which didn't happen too often and certainly hadn't since Karla showed up. Probably for the best. Her true preference was to be a Domme.

Too bad she didn't have anyone challenging enough to play with right now. In the meantime, she offered her services as a Top to anyone requiring or requesting her special skill set—most notably whips and various forms of edge play and sadism. But Grant had zero emotional connection with any of those bottoms.

You had a connection with Liam.

Grant pushed that thought away. For one, there'd never been anything sexual between them, even though she'd been tempted on occasion. The two of them had flirted with danger, but never each other. To further complicate things, she had been his subordinate, and Liam Baxter would never have crossed that line. Besides, she'd never allowed herself to be a Marine mattress for any man. Not in the Marine Corps. Not while private contracting in Iraq and Afghanistan. And not in black ops with Gunnar's Forseti Group.

That rat bastard Liam had gotten her thrown off the team in Afghanistan. For that, she'd never forgive him, assuming they ever met again. It had been nearly five years now, and as far as she knew, Liam had fallen off the face of the earth. Perhaps he'd been killed, but Grant didn't think so.

After licking her wounded pride and reconnecting with her Marines, Adam and Damián, Grant had gone to work for Gunnar.

While he didn't seem to know anything about Liam, Gunnar did know the rival contractor they'd worked for at one time.

Liam was out there somewhere. If only she knew where.

A slow smile came to her lips. Lucky for him she hadn't found him yet. If they ever did meet up again, she'd incapacitate him the way Cassie and Karla had been hanging with ropes earlier—or perhaps a little less delicately—and have his entire body and cock at her mercy.

Hmm. Would she resort to the cock cage, dragon's tail, or something a little more lethal like a knife?

Perhaps all three.

Would consent be involved, or would this be her chance for sweet revenge?

They say that revenge was best served cold. Not true. After all these years, her anger burned hotter than ever. Every time she returned to Afghanistan on a mission for Gunnar, she'd ask around about Liam, certain the bastard wouldn't have been killed during whatever deep undercover work he'd been doing all those years ago.

Unfortunately, their paths had never crossed.

But she'd keep signing up for these Afghan missions. One of these days, she'd find Liam.

And God have mercy on his soul when she did.

About the Author

Kallypso Masters is a *USA Today* Bestselling Author with more than half-a-million copies of her books sold in e-book and paperback formats since August 2011. All her books feature alpha males, strong women, and happy endings because those are her favorite stories to read, but that doesn't mean they don't touch on tough life issues at times. Her original and best-known series—the Rescue Me Saga—features emotional, realistic adult Romance novels with characters healing from past traumas and PTSD, sometimes using unconventional methods (like BDSM).

Kally began publishing *TONY: Slow Burn* and *MATTEO: Wild Fire* her first two of four books in the Raging Fire series, as serials on her Patreon fan club page in spring 2019. Next up will be FRANCO (full title to be determined). From Patreon, the books undergo extensive edits and are then published as ebooks and paperbacks.

An eighth-generation Kentuckian, a few years ago Kally launched the **Bluegrass Spirits** series, supernatural Contemporary Romances set in some of her favorite places in her home state. *Jesse's Hideout* (Bluegrass Spirits #1) takes place in her dad's hometown and includes a recipe section with some of Kally's treasured family recipes, most of which are mentioned in the story. *Kate's Secret* (Bluegrass Spirits #2) takes place in Kentucky's horse country. Local flavor abounds in this series with more books planned in the future.

Kally has been living her own "happily ever after" with her husband of almost 40 years, known affectionately to her readers as Mr. Ray. They have two adult children and an adorable grandson, Erik, who was the model for the character Derek in *Jesse's Hideout* and Erik in

Kate's Secret. (He insisted on having his real name used in the second one!)

Kally enjoys meeting readers wherever she travels and will continue to hold annual KallypsoCons in the United States and Canada as long as she's able. She also likes to cook (most days) and uses the hashtag #CookingAdventuresWithKally on Facebook. To keep up with future events, check out the Appearances or Kally's Events page on her website!

Keep in touch with Kally for updates and much more at kallypso-masters.com/keep-in-touch

To contact or engage with Kally, go to:

Facebook (where almost all of her posts are public),

Facebook Author page,

Patreon Fan Club (for exclusive content/access and serialized stories),

TikTok (tiktok.com/@kallypsomasters)

InstaGram (instagram.com/kallypsomasters), and

Kally's Website (KallypsoMasters.com).

Always feel free to e-mail Kally at kallypsomasters@gmail.com, or write to her at

Kallypso Masters, PO Box 1183, Richmond, KY 40476-1183

Signed Books & Merch in the Kally Store!

Want to own merchandise or personalized, signed paperback copies of any or all of Kallypso Masters' books in the *Rescue Me Saga*, *Rescue Me Saga Extras*, *Bluegrass Spirits*, or the *Raging Fire* series? How about Kallypso Masters Ka-thunk! and and other promotional T-shirts, as well as swag items connected to her books? Kally ships internationally. To shop for these items and much more, go to kallypso masters.com/kally_swag.

And you can also purchase any of Kally's e-books directly from her, too! Go here for a complete list of available titles. New releases will be published exclusively in Kally's Shop before being available on other retailer sites.

kallypsomasters.com/buy-direct

Roar (A Rescue Me Saga Spin-off)

A tragic accident left his beloved wife just beyond his reach, haunting Kristoffer Roar Larson for four years until a chance meeting with Pamela stirs feelings best kept buried. Her assertive alpha personality coupled with her desire to submit and serve fascinates him. Will he allow her presence to shine light once more into the dark corners of his life?

Dr. Pamela Jeffrey thrives on providing medical assistance to those in war-torn corners of the world until a health scare grounds her stateside. While pursuing her deepest secret desire, she encounters Kristoffer, who reluctantly agrees to help prepare her for a future Dom. The bond deepens between them as does her desire for him to be that man in her life, but Kristoffer cannot meet all of her needs. Can she be satisfied with what he can propose without regrets?

As the undeniable connection grows between them, feelings of betrayal take root. How can Pamela convince him he deserves another chance at love? Will Kristoffer be able to fully open himself to the ginger-haired sprite who makes him question everything he once believed? Or will he lose the woman teaching him to live again as surely as he lost the person who first taught him to love?

NOTE: While this book is a standalone, it includes secondary characters from the Rescue Me Saga, including Gunnar Larson, Patrick Gallagher, and V. Grant, and there is a scene in the Masters at Arms Club.

Reading Order for the *Rescue Me Saga & Extras*

kallypsomasters.com/books

Masters at Arms & Nobody's Angel (Combined Volume)

Nobody's Hero

Nobody's Perfect

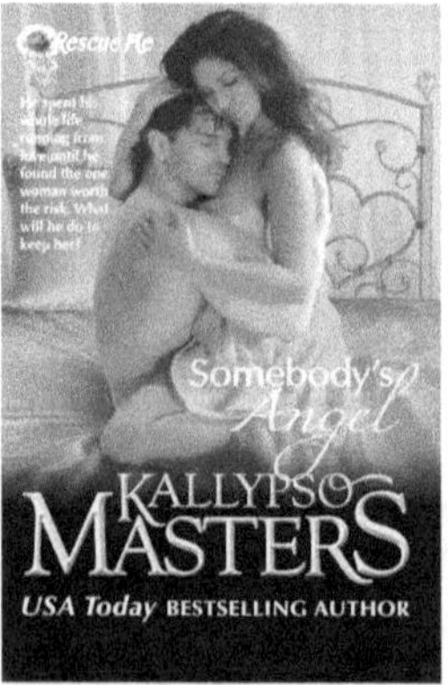

Somebody's Angel

Nobody's Lost

Nobody's Dream

Western Dreams

Somebody's Perfect

Wedding Dreams

Forever Bound

Reading Order for the *Raging Fire* Series

TONY: Slow Burn

MATTEO: Wild Fire